KILLER PICTURES

HOPE MADDEN

World Castle Publishing, LLC
Pensacola, Florida
Copyright © 2025 Hope Madden
Paperback ISBN: 9798891263673
eBook ISBN: 9798891263680
First Edition World Castle Publishing, LLC, June 17, 2025
http://www.worldcastlepublishing.com
Licensing Notes
Cover: Cover Designs by Karen
Editor: Karen Fuller

CHAPTER ONE

The squelching sound made her cringe more than the images on the screen. She squinted to see those better. Destiny Arnold was not the kind of person to turn away from the sight of a hugely pregnant woman, face smeared with blood, crouching in the corner of a filthy basement, feasting on a carcass.

Nope. This was right up her alley, generally. And though she had to admit that the sound design here was…well…it was noticeable. It was noteworthy — yes, it was noteworthy — she wasn't so sure the balance of the film merited an audience at Madness and Mayhem Film Festival.

Still, she watched the whole thing. Every minute of it. Because a ton of people worked really hard to make *Metamorphosis*, and even if they did a mainly terrible job, they deserved to have their whole film seen.

"Don't you think?" she asked Church, the large, dark gray cat shedding on her Muppet pajama pants. He smelled like Doritos.

She brushed orange dust from her furry companion, then peeked back at the movie when she heard the grunting and screaming. Church hopped onto the bare dining room table, his eyes the only thing you could see behind the light from the laptop screen. It gave Dez a sickly pallor, that light, while the rest of her empty dining room remained hidden in the dark.

She winced as the woman onscreen held a giant, gooey, squirming larva as if holding a beloved newborn. Dez pulled the mainly unwilling cat back to her lap.

"At least she's not alone, amirite?"

Dez didn't start at all when her phone buzzed. She turned it face down and hugged the cat closer. It buzzed again, and Church mewed a little tragically. Then came the doorbell.

"Maybe we just won't answer," she

whispered. Dez hugged the reluctant cat close to her face. The phone buzzed again. And then a knock. Then she heard "I know you're home" from outside the door. "Where else would you be? Give me back my cat."

Dez abandoned the laptop and walked, cat dangling, to the door. Yolanda stood, hair wild, arms out for Church.

"Oh, you're home." Dez had no skill in delivering false emotion. She tried, but her fake smile gave her the look of a dialed-down lunatic. She handed over the cat, then gathered up some toys scattered around the dark floor: a bold pink shoestring, a green ball with a bell inside, and a tiny Chucky doll.

She felt like she should ask Yolanda … something.

"Did you guys have a good time?" That was a good question. That was totally normal.

Yolanda nuzzled the cat.

"Well, I did not murder my husband. And we're still married." She held one raincoat pocket open for Dez to fill with Church's toys. "Life is not like the movies, you know?"

Dez suddenly pictured Yolanda eating her husband's carcass and cradling Church in a larva suit.

"Anyway," Yolanda said, squirmy cat under her arm, "thanks for keeping him. The kid's asleep in the car, so I need to scoot."

Dez closed the door behind Yolanda and returned to her laptop. After she watched the last credit—and held back a snicker as text on the screen announced, "You have just witnessed a Metamorphosis!"—she minimized, brought up the rating rubric, and typed: *Story asks why we want to be scared before literally giving birth to horror. A fine underpinning for a horror film.*

"Just not this one," she said to the empty house. She typed again: *Good effort, but not a great fit for the festival.*

About to shut the lid for the day because it was very late and she couldn't remember if she'd eaten anything other than

Doritos, Dez saw a new title pop up at the top of the list of submitted movies: *Adam*.

"*Adam*, eh?"

She hovered the mouse over the title. Her eyes already kind of burned and she for sure needed to pee. For sure.

"It's a short one, though…"

Dez clicked play.

Gauzy curtains blew. A hand in black leather gloves lifted the window. Inside, a woman danced, her silhouette obscured by the shining dark hair falling over her features, grazing her shoulder. Was there another figure in the distance?

Dez dug the whole Dario Argento vibe and appreciated the way the camerawork drew her in. She heard his laugh, this mystery man in the distance. As the woman tossed her shirt his way, the tattoo of a lizard climbed her ribcage.

Dez got comfortable just as it seemed the gloved marauder had made it all the way into the house. And then it was over. Done. Black screen. No credits, nothing.

"That's it?"

She clicked around the festival platform, looking for some explanation, but could find no actual information about the film. No filmmakers to contact, nothing. She thought about watching it again, then eyed the rest of the titles waiting for her attention.

Dez absently scratched a deep suicide-correct scar running down her wrist.

"Too many movies," she said, stretching, cat hair and Dorito powder clinging to her pajama pants. "I am never going to survive this film festival."

***

Next morning, the laptop relocated from her empty dining room to her empty home office. Dez sported makeup, combed hair, and a clean button-down—and scuzzy Muppet pajama pants, not that anyone on Zoom could tell.

She clicked the 'allow video' icon and waited, her insincere smile hovering above the Destiny Arnold label. Yolanda's beaming face appeared on the screen, her hair barely contained by the edges of the frame. It wasn't as if Yolanda still clung to the 1980s. Her hair was simply meant for that decade.

"Morning, D," Yolanda said. Before Dez had to think of a response, a grinning, densely bearded face materialized over the name Adam Vivod. His big, sweet smile no longer seemed ill-fitting to Dez. She liked the disconnect between his lovely personality and his Cannibal Corpse shirt collection.

It took him a minute to get his audio working, then he sing-songed, "Hellllo."

Yolanda pointed to her Twin Peaks coffee mug.

"Hey, my coffee's depleted," she said. "Amuse yourselves while I refill, yeah?"

Dez stared at the empty space where Yolanda had been, worrying for a second about the inevitable awkward silence when she remembered.

"Hey, Adam!" she said. "Did you see that movie? The one in the queue? Called Adam?"

Adam's look was of delightful surprise.

"No! There is one?"

"There is!" Dez confirmed. "That's the title. It's not great…it doesn't seem finished, I guess. It's like it could be an Argento remake of *Body Double*."

Adam's face implied intrigue, but the conversation was cut off when Yolanda returned, and Howie joined. Yolanda was clearly texting as she greeted him, "Morning, handsome."

Howie grinned modestly, and then, on Dez's phone, the message: *there's your boyyyyyy*

Dez pretended not to notice.

"Grant can't make it," Yolanda announced to the group. "He just arrived in Mexico at Fantasma with his own movie, and the timing didn't work out," she said, holding her phone up and squinting. "He left a message. Always the artistic leader."

She smiled, then read: "I like what I'm seeing in these submissions, but I don't love it. The best horror filmmakers are the ones who can't be trusted. The ones who make you believe they are not interested in your wellbeing. If you watch a movie and know in your gut that the children aren't really in peril, or there really will be a final girl, instead of whatever scares you most, the filmmaker has failed. We're not looking for failures."

Yolanda nodded, then tried to swig her coffee, set down her phone, and share her screen simultaneously. The phone clattered, and the coffee sloshed, but it was overall a success. The film festival judging site overtook the screen, and Yolanda said, "Looks like some folks have seen *Metamorphosis, Dick Eaters,* and *Meatboat.*"

"Meatboat!" the entire team shouted in unison.

"Thoughts?" Yolanda asked.

Adam's image took over most of the screen as he talked, and Dez's eye sought the thumbnail image of Howie.

"I really liked all three," Adam

finished, stroking his beard. Dez had missed whatever else he had to say, but she noticed disagreement on Howie's face. Then she wondered how long she might have been looking at Howie. Could people tell? She looked at everyone's little square and tried to figure out what they were looking at. Adam kept talking, but she didn't hear him.

Yolanda's bzzz brought her around. *Adam likes everything*, the text read.

Dez tried to conceal her fingering and messaged back: *too nice to be a judge.* Feeling guilty, she looked back at Adam, determined to pay attention.

"And even though they were pretty gory," he was saying, "they had some great themes."

Howie laughed. Howie had such a great laugh. Big. "I think I missed the themes."

"They might have been drowned out by the sound of eating," Yolanda offered.

Smiles crossed all the faces on the screen except Adam's.

"I mean, did she have to eat him?" Yolanda howled. "I draw the line at cannibalism. They can eat me — that is their prerogative. But I won't eat a person."

"No better way to dispose of a dead body," Dez offered. She almost froze as she heard herself say it, but with this particular group of people, talk like that was accepted without a thought. In fact, Yolanda laughed even louder.

Then Howie asked, "What about *Meatboat*?" and everyone yelled out, "MEATBOAT!"

"How do you let that many people die and still end up the hero?" Howie continued with that saucy laugh.

Adam, always a little more thoughtful than the rest, responded, "I think the filmmaker was saying that you have to forgive yourself if you want to survive."

Murmurs and nods suggested reluctant agreement from the team.

"Real quick," Yolanda brought the group back to attention. "The fest hired a new marketing firm to help bolster attendance this year."

Her shared screen went to the marketing group's website: *Killer Pictures. We make nightmares come true.*

She scrolled past images that looked like behind-the-scenes shots, others of massive lines circling movie theaters, others of likely colleagues looking at laptops, and one of a solidly built man in a suit and a man bun talking into a megaphone in front of a crowd.

"I don't think we need them, actually," Yolanda admitted. "And I thought, maybe if we had some ideas that might help market the festival, we could throw them around here, and I could share them."

"Maybe something to draw media attention," Howie offered. "Like a stunt."

Dez had a thought to share. "We should throw stuff off the theater roof."

She could tell from the way Adam lit up that he agreed.

"Like condoms filled with red Jell-O,"

he suggested. "Or a mannequin head!"

"Filled with red Jell-O!" Dez returned.

Howie's turn: "Whole mannequins filled with red Jell-O!"

"Would we move the cars?" Adam wondered.

"No!" the entire screen of faces responded.

Dez could see it in her head: limbs and viscera and lifeless, frozen faces, cars mangled from the impact. She shuddered, but, eyeing the Brady Bunch zoom frames, brightened at the smiles and camaraderie.

Yolanda shrugged. "We are getting off target. Wrapping up so I can get Michael over to preschool. Dez, we need a tiebreaker vote on *Meatboat*."

As Yolanda closed out the meeting, Dez joined in a unison chant: "Meatboat!"

Adam added quickly, "I'll check out *Adam*."

"Remember, it's not great," Dez warned him. "Although the naked dancer has this badass tattoo, like a lizard climbing up her ribcage."

It surprised Dez the abrupt way Adam's smile disappeared as she clicked out of the meeting.

***

Later that morning, still wearing the pajama pant/dress shirt combo, Dez typed away at a spreadsheet. No music played. No photos or mementos decorated the desk or walls. The blinds were low, the laptop screen was the main source of light in the room until her phone screen lit up with the word GRACE. Dez saw it, but she let it go to voicemail before listening.

"Hey, lady! Want to help me make Maude's costume? It's complicated. You'll suck, but it will be fun."

Before Dez could decide whether she did or did not want to attempt elementary school Halloween costumery, she felt more buzzing. Her phone was suddenly alight with texts from Yolanda.

OMG!!

Oh my god

For real Oh my god
WTF? Are you even seeing this?
I can't even

Dez liked that Yolanda never seemed able to collect her thoughts. She also felt a bit overwhelmed and dizzy because of it sometimes. She texted back: *What is up?*

Yolanda called.

"What's the deal?" Dez asked.

"Adam!!" was Yolanda's startlingly loud answer.

"Did you watch it?" Dez asked, assuming Yolanda was talking about the film submission. "I didn't think much of it."

***

From her seat on the floor in a homey living room, warmly lit and littered with action figures, Yolanda pieced together Legos on a glass tabletop. Her 4-year-old struggled to separate a red block from a yellow, so his mom reached across to help.

"I cannot believe he did it."

"Did what?" Dez asked.

"Holy lord!" was the response, and

Yolanda hoisted herself up from the floor and walked toward the open kitchen to put some space between her mouth and little ears.

She smiled at Michael and pointed to the separated blocks, like 'keep yourself busy,' when Dez asked again: "What are you talking about?!"

Yolanda grabbed a URL and texted it to Dez. "Watch it," Yolanda ordered nonchalantly. "I'm just heading out to pick up Michael's costume. I'll stop over."

"Hey, Mark," Yolanda called, unsure where to even focus her voice. "Hey, I'm heading to Target for a costume that actually fits Michael." She could not believe he thought his own son wouldn't split the seams on last year's Boba Fett suit. "Keep an eye on the wee one, yeah?"

She smiled at Michael, and when he smiled back and used a Lego hand to wave goodbye, Yolanda came in for a hug.

"I'll be right back," she told him. "Listen to Daddy while I'm gone. And make good decisions. Make Captain America decisions."

"I will," he answered with a Lego-hand salute.

***

Dez walked her phone to the charger, plugged it in, and sat on the floor next to it. She clicked the link Yolanda sent—a clip from the local news. A newscaster—Dez recognized him from his "on your side" coverage ads—stood on the front lawn of some suburban house surrounded by police tape. Dez didn't know the house, figured it was some true crime thing she wouldn't be interested in, and nearly clicked out until she heard On Your Side say, "Ellen Vivod never made it to work this morning."

"Vivod?"

On Your Side turned to an elderly man, his arm being tugged by a dog leash. Maybe two. The newscaster continued, "According to neighbor Arthur Poignon, when he and his two dachshunds left for their morning walk, he heard her screaming."

On Your Side held his microphone out. Arthur Poignon surprised the newscaster by taking the microphone with his free hand. He spoke slowly.

"The girls got to barking," he nodded, first at On Your Side, then at the camera. "There was shouting."

Mr. Poignon looked sadly down at the dogs.

"Then it was quiet, and Mr. V opened the door."

Arthur Poignon's head nodded slightly with each sentence as if acknowledging to himself the truth of what he'd seen. Behind him, the perfectly benign house—beige siding, white shutters, a little American flag on the mailbox, curtains blowing along the side of the building—looked like anything other than the scene of a crime. As usual.

"He was bloody," Mr. Poignon nodded. "He smiled at my dogs."

Mr. Poignon looked up at On Your Side, whose expression was the frozen image of interest.

"And he...he just...he cut his own throat open."

"Oh my God..." Dez gasped, her focus floating to the police tape. Did she see blue and red lights? No, that couldn't be right. It was daylight out. Not like the other time, red and blue swirling across townies, worried little sister Grace in her Doc Martens, their dad, the silver inside of the ambulance door.

Dez's bony butt was weary from sitting on the bare floor, so she tipped onto her side, felt the cold of the floor on her hot face, and rested that way until the doorbell.

Sometime later—Dez wasn't really sure how much later—she and Yolanda sat side by side on her front porch. It had never occurred to Dez to put porch chairs out, so they sat on the bare concrete with their feet on the steps. Dez could smell a fire pit. It smelled like fall. Like neighbors.

"When something like this happens, people are always like, 'Oh, they seemed so happy,'" Yolanda said. "But I'm serious, Destiny, they were happy. Adam and Ellen were all like chili cook-offs and wave at your neighbors nice."

Dez nodded. She pretended for a second she would someday wave at a neighbor. She'd only met Adam in person one time, so she didn't have a solid opinion about him that would sound insightful.

"He was so smiley," she said. Best she could do, but Yolanda nodded in agreement. Then, looking at Yolanda, she said, "You are also very smiley. Are you going to kill someone?"

"I might," Yolanda said. "You've met my husband, right?"

Dez nodded. That checked out.

"We know a murderer," Yolanda said, staring blankly, straight ahead. She paused, then: "I kind of want to get to know Mr. Poignon."

"Those dogs!" Dez clapped.

"'The girls!'" Yolanda mimicked. "Also, Arthur is a great name."

Dez nodded. "I bet he has dishes of hard candies all around his house."

Smiling, Yolanda got up to leave. She stretched a bit and took a step toward her newish minivan—the one with a SpongeBob decal and *The Shining* carpet-patterned seat covers.

"You're watching some films today, yeah?" she asked before getting in. "I hate to say it like this, but we are now down a judge."

Dez shrugged, resigned to it. "Sure."

CHAPTER TWO

Dez finished some actual work—data mining, which was boring as hell, but she could do it from home without ever having to shower, shave, or meet with, see, or talk to anybody and risk being herself. She unplugged her laptop and carried it to the dining room table to be closer to the fridge.

She clicked on the film site and scrolled through the titles:

Kaleidoscope of Horror
Hatred by Number

Nothing jumped out at her. The dining room chair was hard and cold, and Dez thought about grabbing a blanket. She should just turn the heat on. Then she noticed something. She looked closely. She scrolled up and down.

No *Adam*.

Dez did something she didn't usually

do. She initiated contact. She texted Yolanda: *Did you delete Adam?*

Almost immediately, Yolanda texted back: *His account? No. Should I?*

Dez gave her phone a disgusted look and said out loud, "No, you idiot."

She started to text a reply but wasn't sure how to make it make sense, so she called.

"No, you remember the short film called *Adam*?" she explained the second Yolanda answered. "It's not here anymore."

"I don't remember a film called *Adam*," Yolanda yawned.

"Well, it was here, and now it's gone. How weird is that?"

It was weird. It was super weird, right? Couldn't Yolanda see that it was weird?

"Maybe they withdrew?" Yolanda offered, but Dez wasn't paying attention anymore. She was scrolling, and in her effort, she noticed a film called *Grant*.

"No way..." she half-whispered.

Her phone buzzed. The screen lit up with the word GRACE. She pushed it to voicemail and looked back at the laptop screen.

"You still there?" Yolanda asked.

Quickly, Dez offered, "Yeah, sorry. I'll let you go. Going to watch some movies."

"Good girl," Yolanda replied, but Dez didn't quite hear her as she hovered over the film *Grant* and clicked play.

***

In the hazy afternoon light, two figures stand side by side on a homey front lawn. A little girl in a green dress reaches up and takes the hand of a handsome man beside her. It looks like he's holding a small suitcase, sized for the child, in his other hand, but as the camera moves closer, the case takes shape. It's a record player, the kind with a lid that latches.

The handsome man sets the record player on the ground and holds his hand out toward the camera.

"Comeon, son," hesaysencouragingly.

The handsome man shakes his head and looks down at the little girl. She's maybe 5 or 6, her thin, sandy hair pulled back in a green ribbon to match her dress, wispy bangs hanging in her eyes. She scratches her nose.

The handsome man looks again at the camera and sighs. He stoops to pick up the record player, and he and the little girl turn their backs to the camera. They walk slowly, ghostlike, to the wide, wooden front porch of a sturdy house.

He sets the record player down on the porch. Opens it. Taped to the inside of the lid are Polaroids: the little girl and a small boy.

Handsome man drops the needle on a 45-record sitting on the turntable. He turns back to the camera.

"Come on, son," he says, more sad now than encouraging. "Don't make her dance all alone."

The camera moves backward as if stumbling, providing a better view of the house. On the porch the little girl dances sadly as the handsome man watches. She holds both hands out as if holding a partner. She steps forward, back, forward, back.

The handsome man claps, and she stops. He moves the needle, closes and latches the record player lid. He stands, the record player in hand, looks at the camera, and beckons.

He opens the front door to the house, takes the little girl by the hand, and walks inside.

The film cuts to an interior. In a dusty, empty room, light spills through naked windows toward an open closet door. Rope is piled on the floor of the closet.

The little girl looks at the floor, her hands worrying the green edges of her skirt.

Handsome Man pulls a pocketknife from his back pocket, unfolds it slowly, and looks back at the camera with a sly smile. Then he stoops and uses the knife to wedge open slats in the floor. Again, he looks at the camera, this time grinning mischievously.

"You never did know where I kept the treasure hidden, did you, buddy?"

The handsome man chuckles to himself as he pulls up the boards and slides the record player into the hole. Light from the window glints off a stack of images — Polaroids, mostly. Tough to tell, but it looks like pictures of two children, with more photos stacked next to film reels and a Super 8 camera.

The handsome man replaces the floorboards and then reaches for the sad little girl, still frozen in place a few paces away. She walks to him, and he affectionately rubs her small head. He holds her little face in his hands, looks her in the eye, and nods.

The sad little girl nods back, walks into the closet, picks up a rope from the floor, and fastens a noose.

She and Handsome Man look toward the camera.

Fade to black.

***

"That was unsettling," Dez said to no

one.

She minimized the screen for the movie and scrolled to a rating rubric. She looked again at the title: *Grant*.

"What is with these titles? Who is Grant?" she wondered. "The man? The boy in the photos? The film festival judge who never shows up to our Zoom calls?"

Her ponderings were interrupted by the buzz of her phone. Yolanda. She answered.

"Hey."

"I just got off the phone with Joshua," Yolanda told her.

"Film festival Joshua? Mr. Joshua? Why? Did he find a judge to fill in for Adam?"

Dez pushed back from the table and wandered toward the fridge, not really sure why this required a phone call. She'd think of it as human interaction practice. As she opened the door for another can of Diet Pepsi, Yolanda informed her, "Destiny, Grant is in the hospital." Her voice was hushed but dramatic.

"What?"

Then, more quietly, "He got shot."

"What??!!!" Dez dropped the can. "What happened?"

She stooped to collect the can, sitting it in her crusty stainless-steel sink as Yolanda explained.

"He broke into somebody's house, and they shot him."

Dez looked around her empty house at no one and nothing, astonished.

"No way!"

"He got back from Mexico tonight, drove to this house, broke in with an ax, and got shot by a neighbor. Joshua didn't say a lot more," Yolanda reported.

"Oh my God ... an ax?!!" Dez immediately moved to the laptop and Googled 'Grant Arbogast' but found nothing. Then 'Columbus ax break in,' and still nothing.

"There's nothing online about it," Dez said.

"D, it just happened," Yolanda clarified.

Dez closed the laptop lid and stood. Stalking aimlessly, she absently picked up the can of pop and opened it. It exploded all over the button-down and Muppet pajama pants. Dez dropped the can back into the sink and grabbed for a towel but wondered aloud, "How did Joshua Brose know about it already?"

She listened and dabbed her shirt with a dish towel before just giving up and stripping it off. She used the shirt rather than the towel to wipe up the mess on the floor, then realized and threw it, exasperated. She dropped her ass on the floor and just sat.

"The house is right there by the theater," Yolanda was saying. "We were on the phone while he was driving home from work, and the road was blocked. He just asked somebody what happened..."

"Why were you on the phone with Joshua Brose? Is he planning to cancel the festival?"

Yolanda paused. "No. That's not why. But he did tell me that I should stop watching the submitted movies altogether. So maybe he is thinking about canceling it now."

Dez hopped up from the sticky floor and moved back to her laptop, wiping her hands on wet Muppet faces. She refreshed Google, asking Yolanda, "It was a house by the theater? Which house?"

Channel 4 had posted news footage. Dez clicked the link to find the same newscaster from the Adam Vivod coverage standing in a lonesome front yard, exactly where the handsome man had stood with the sad little girl in the movie *Grant*.

"No way..."

The house looked a little different than it had in the film, especially with the police tape announcing the spot as a crime scene.

"God, that is so fucking weird," Dez said to herself and then to Yolanda, "Are you watching this?"

She texted her the link. Meanwhile, On Your Side looked dramatically into the camera as if to draw Dez into his soliloquy.

"Like the movies he makes, Grant Arbogast's final moments on earth may be nothing but horror," he reported, then walked toward the porch. Dez spied several officers exiting the building, including one in plain clothes with a badge on a chain around her neck. Dez decided Badge-on-Chain was in charge and then immediately wondered whether movies had put that idea into her head.

The reporter continued ominously, "Local filmmaker Grant Arbogast broke into this house," he said with a toss of his head. "The very home where Arbogast himself had grown up."

Too nutty…

Footage changed to close-ups of the porch, menacing teeth of broken glass circled the windowpane, as the reporter's voice narrated: "Neighbors heard glass breaking and saw a man with an ax and a gas can breaking into the home. One neighbor called the police while another set out to investigate, a loaded handgun in his jacket pocket."

A series of still photos on the screen depicted the scene: the same front room from the film *Grant*, this time with an ax driven into the floor, a spilled gas can, circles made in chalk around footprints and ax marks, Post-it notes stuck here and there.

As Dez strained to take it all in, she listened to the reporter.

"Arbogast is in critical condition at Sisters of Mercy Hospital."

Dez pointed to the screen and announced to Yolanda, still on the line, "That's the house from the movie."

"What movie?"

And though no one could see her, Dez waved her hand excitedly.

"The *Grant* movie!"

But Yolanda was lost. "Which one of his movies? Did he film there?"

Dez clicked on the film festival site.

"Not one of his movies," she answered, distracted and scrolling. "One for judging. The short in the queue called *Grant*. It's totally shot at that same house."

Dez squinted, realizing something.

"The same thing happened to Adam."

"Stop mumbling," Yolanda requested. She seemed a little checked out of this conversation. Before Dez could respond, her doorbell rang. She jumped.

Who was at her door? Why would anyone be at her door? She thought of Grant Arbogast sneaking around, weapon in hand.

The bell rang again.

"Fuck." She whispered into the phone as she hung up, "I have to get the door."

Dez slunk through the dark and rarely used living room toward her front door. She imagined a screeching Bernard Herrmann score serenading her mounting dread, then breathed. No, Dez knew she was not destined to be Marion Crane. Most of her life was spent trying not to be Norman Bates.

She got on tiptoes to sneak a peek

through the high window. A hand flipping the bird hit the glass in front of her. She laughed, relieved, and opened up.

Grace, Dez's freckle-faced younger sister—a smaller, similar looking woman but pregnant—stood on Dez's front porch smiling, canvas grocery bags hanging on both arms. She pushed past Dez and into the house.

"You're not answering."

CHAPTER THREE

Grace looked around the living room, judging. No TV yet, not one light on, and the only chair in the room was piled high with laundry. This didn't look good. She handed the bags to her sister and opened some window shades.

"I'm fine," Dez told her.

Grace nodded, disbelieving, and noticed Dez absently pinching the scar on her arm. Grace looked tenderly at her sister. "Maude wants you to trick-or-treat with us."

Dez didn't respond right away, and Grace couldn't quite read her face, so she continued walking through the house, flipping on lights and looking for clues. Dez followed.

"Really," Dez half pleaded. "I'm fine." But her sister was unconvinced. Grace turned to face her.

"I think this movie festival thing was a bad idea."

Dez sighed.

"You spend more time alone now than you did before you moved back."

"It's a lot of movies to get through," she explained. "I'm not avoiding people on purpose."

"Uh huh," Grace muttered over her shoulder as she moved toward the kitchen. "Your old doctor said you were ready to make friends. Have you made any friends? Don't make any up—I'll know by their pretend names."

Dez laughed. Grace pulled what was left of a roast and some big Tupperware containers—leftovers, but better than Pop-Tarts and Doritos—out of her bag and laid them out on the counter.

"Yolanda is my friend."

"Horror movie tattoos and bad marriage—that one?" Grace asked.

Dez nodded. She grabbed zip lock

bags and a large cutting board from a cupboard, unasked, and set them on the counter where her sister worked portioning boiled potatoes and carrots into smaller plastic containers and popping the lids on. It smelled tasty, even cold.

Grace stopped.

"She doesn't remind you of anybody, though, right? Nobody from back home?"

Dez picked at her scar. "No."

"You can't keep letting your mind go back there."

"I know."

"I don't know why you always want to go back there. There is terrible."

"I don't *want* to go…"

But she did, though. Grace knew it, and that was the rub. But one step at a time.

"She's nice, Yolanda? You need good friends. Nice friends."

Dez seemed to think about it.

"Nice-ish," she said. "She's funny."

Grace clapped her hands, happy.

"Good enough. Funny is good."

She handed small containers to Dez, who piled them in the fridge. Then Grace took the chopping board and held her hand out for a knife. Dez fished a carving knife from a drawer between them and handed it to her sister, who began carving off big pieces of roast beef, individually packaging them in zip lock bags and stacking them on the counter.

"Put a couple in the freezer. They'll go bad if they sit in the fridge for too long. This way, you'll have something for next week, too," she told Dez. She set the knife down neatly and nodded. "Don't you feel like chocolate milk?" Grace asked, heading for Dez's fridge to grab a half gallon of white milk, then nabbed some cocoa powder from the cupboard.

"I didn't get it for you," Dez pointed to the cocoa powder. "I got it for your daughter."

"Well, it's mine now!" Grace laughed a quietly sinister chuckle. "Mwa hahaha."

As Grace started pouring, Dez grabbed

the bags of meat and disappeared down the basement steps. When she returned, she looked solemnly at her sister.

"So, well, maybe I'm not 100% fine."

Grace turned, concerned, maybe angry.

"I knew it."

"Did you see that guy, Adam Vivod, who killed his wife and himself?" Dez began.

"No," Grace answered, handing her beverage to her sister and, with some effort, pulling herself to sit on the counter. She held her hand out for her drink. "That is quite a name, by the way."

"I knew him," Dez said.

"No way!"

"I did," Dez continued. "He was one of the film festival judges."

Grace took a swig, fascinated. "And you know you had nothing to do with the murder," she stated plainly.

Dez looked irritated. "Of course not!"

"You didn't cause it," Grace continued, evenly. "You couldn't have prevented it..."

Grace was careful not to sound robotic because Dez hated that. But she never altered her gaze. She looked steadily and calmly into Destiny's face. Dez stepped away from her sister.

"I know that."

Grace accepted this.

"Right," she said. "Just checking. Go on."

Dez sat on the counter next to her sister. It made Grace think of being kids, parking next to each other in the kitchen while their dad made them pancakes for dinner, or omelets. Nothing beat eating breakfast food for dinner.

"One of the other judges just broke into somebody's house with an ax and got shot."

"Shut up!" Grace laughed from shock.

Dez seemed to relax a bit. "I swear to God."

"OK," Grace slapped her sister on the knee. It was time. "So, you are definitely quitting the film festival." This was manageable chaos, and Grace needed to get back home to make sure Maude finished her math homework. She sniffed in the air at her sister. "Maybe showering..."

Dez crossed her arms in front of her and slid off the counter.

"Get out of your house tomorrow," Grace continued. "Perhaps say hello to a neighbor. Probably not a bad idea to find a local doc."

Dez sighed heavily, and Grace looked at her, frowning.

"You were doing so well."

"Dude, it's fine," Dez reassured her.

Was it? Please, please, please let it be fine.

"Come with me tomorrow," Grace suggested, holding her hand out for Dez to help her off the counter. "Bring your laptop, you can work at my house while I finish the baby's room."

"You only want me there to put stuff on the high shelves you can't reach."

"That is entirely true," Grace smiled.

She set her empty glass in the sink, ran water in it, and hugged her sister. Dez rested her chin on Grace's head, and Grace soaked in her warmth. As they separated, Grace continued advising: "Speak to a living human tomorrow."

Dez pointed to Grace's ample belly.

"Look how fast you keep making people, though," she said. "I mean, how many humans do I need to know?"

"I do make the best ones," Grace nodded, hugging her own girth with satisfaction. "Still, you should do some of the work. Talk to somebody non-related tomorrow."

Dez grimaced, and the two walked toward the door.

"And quit that film festival," Grace commanded. "Do it!"

***

Dez was up. That was something. She had slept really late, like lunchtime late, and was feeling pretty good. She couldn't remember the last time she just went to bed and didn't sit up all hours watching horror. And now she planned to change out of her Muppet pajama pants, put on real pants. Maybe shoes. But there it was, right where she left it, gleaming its silvery shine right at her. Dez stared for a long while at that laptop, then yielded to a return rendezvous with the Handsome Man.

"Come on, son."

Dez paused the short film and pulled Howie up in her texts. He was non-related. He counted, right? After tapping her thumbs nervously on the side of the phone for an excruciating amount of time, she mustered her courage and just called.

He answered. "Hello?"

Dez stumbled. "Hi. I, hi. It's Dez. Destiny Arnold. From the festival."

"I can see that," he chuckled. "What's up?"

What is up? Why did she do this? Dez stood and stepped nervously from foot to stockinged foot.

"Did you ever watch that *Grant*

short?" she asked him, suddenly serious.

"I did," he said, which surprised her with a feeling of relief. "It was weird. Hardly horror. I liked it, though."

"You heard about Grant, though?" she asked. "I mean, our Grant—the actual guy? At the house, with the ax and the neighbor and the gun."

"Yes," he said. "Horrible."

That was it. That was all her brain was willing to give her to say out loud to anyone. To a boy. To a cute boy. Panic began to rise. Nothing came out of her mouth. Because what was she going to say now? *Huh, isn't that nutty?* Or maybe, *I think a movie made him do it.* Mercifully, Howie broke the silence.

"Hey, I was just going to get some food. Do you want to come?"

Dez winced and shook her head no. But she thought about what Grace said, and took a deep, cleansing breath. She nodded.

"Um, yeah," she said, so smooth. "Should I meet you?"

"Give me 15," he said. "I'll come get

you."

Dez hung up and smiled for one instant before looking down to see herself in her cruddy pajama pants. She dashed to the shower.

***

Her hair was still wet as she belted herself into Howie's off-red Honda. She smiled at Howie, not knowing if the moment was dreamy or awkward until Lester — Howie's chocolate lab — poked his head up from the back seat. Dez nuzzled the square little brown noggin she'd only glimpsed in Zoom calls.

"Lesterrrrrr," she gushed, rubbing everything she could reach from the front seat. He smelled like dog. Lester needed a bath. "We finally meet in person."

Howie reached over and tugged absently on her seatbelt to make sure it was hooked. She blushed. She realized she probably smelled like a dog now, too, and used all her might not to sniff her hands. That would be unseemly, right? Yes. Definitely bad.

"Really crazy about Grant," Howie said, pulling out.

They rode in awkward silence for a few minutes, but the day was bright, and the leaves were brighter, their wild oranges and yellows catching the sun, and Dez felt relaxed. Still, a thought was running through her head, and since Howie had seen the short film, why not ask him?

"Right," she said out loud, although it was meant for herself. "So that house, though? The one in the movie called *Grant*? That's the house Grant Arbogast broke into with an ax and a gas can."

Howie swerved. Dez instinctively grabbed the door handle for safety.

"No, it isn't!" He looked at her, maybe longer than she was comfortable with. He was operating a vehicle, after all. "Are you serious?"

The dreamy haze rubbed clear. Dez closed her eyes and breathed in, out, slow, steady.

"I just watched it again," she said calmly. "It's definitely the same house."

She opened her eyes. His eyes were back on the road. She let go of the door and turned to face him. This was serious. Was this serious? Maybe not.

"It was his own house, right?" she began. "That's what they said on the news. So, some filmmaker just made a movie called *Grant* set at the house where Grant Arbogast grew up, and then Grant Arbogast watched that movie, broke into the house, and got shot."

Howie turned the wheel onto a side street, looking ahead. He agreed. "That's fucked up right there."

Encouraged, Dez pulled out her phone and clicked the film site link, saying, "I feel like there has to be a way to see who made the movie."

She looked up at him, proud of her good thinking, but he returned her glance with a bit of worry.

"Can't tell?" he asked.

Dez returned her focus to the phone. There didn't seem to be any additional data with the film—no filmmaker names, no email address, no larger site to link to, no social links. How was the festival even supposed to reach out if the movie was selected? She shook her head.

"I don't know. Either they didn't post the information, or it's maybe hidden?"

"Hmmm. Too bad," Howie commiserated.

Dez dropped her phone in her lap, frustrated. "Maybe Yolanda can see it."

"I don't know," Howie responded.

Pulling into a Chipotle parking lot, Howie nodded.

"Is this OK?" he asked, unbuckling his seatbelt. "You like Mexican?"

Dez was elated.

"I am dangerously fond of Mexican food."

Howie was smiling, the sun was warm in the front seat, and Lester's panting gave rhythm and life to the whole little world.

She kind of wanted to just stay. She kind of wanted to reach across Howie for the lever that adjusted his seat and see if she could fit her body between him and the steering wheel. A hot flush crossed her face.

Howie smiled at her. "Thanks for coming."

She answered appropriately: "Thanks for asking."

Howie rolled his window down a bit for Lester, who sprawled comfortably across the backseat and got out of the car.

"We'll bring you back a steak bowl, buddy."

Alone with the dog for a beat, Dez exhaled and exited the vehicle.

They ordered burritos and ate in the car so Lester wouldn't be lonely. The burrito kept her hands full, so no worries where they might go. Nothing turned sour; her belly was full, and Howie's crooked bottom teeth made her happily dizzy.

He dropped her at her house. Heading up to the door she noticed a Target bag tucked under a nearly naked bush by her porch. Dez looked inside: Halloween candy and a costume. Maybe a pirate? She took a picture and texted it to Yolanda.

Yolanda responded: *THANK GOD! Looking everywhere!*

Dez chuckled, happy to help. *Oh, what the hell*, she thought, kind of proud of herself. She texted: *will drop it by*

"Look at me," she said out loud, tucking the bag under her arm. "Making human contact left and right today. Who needs a doctor?"

***

The drive to Yolanda's took ten minutes, according to Dez's phone. It didn't require any highway driving. The highway route would only have saved her three minutes, and there was plenty of time before trick or treat. It was too early for much traffic. Plus, Dez was in a peaceful mood and had a full belly. The drive wasn't even traumatizing.

Directions dropped her at a big,

homey place very decorated for the season. Inflatables drooped across the lawn, waiting for evening power to fill with air and frighten. Dez wondered what each would plump up to become. Lots of white puddles of plastic, so she guessed ghosts but hoped maybe one was a Stay Puft Marshmallow Man because she suddenly realized how perfect he would be as an inflatable lawn decoration.

She stood next to Yolanda's hanging red porch swing and knocked. The main door was open, so she peered through the glass of the storm door through an entryway and an open kitchen all the way to a family room where the overhead lamp reflected on a big, square glass table. Yolanda popped out of somewhere back there when Dez knocked.

"Whew!" Yolanda pantomimed, wiping her brow as she opened the door and eyed the bag, which Dez held proudly out in front of her. "Now Michael won't have to make do with these devil horns I wore to last year's Halloween party."

Yolanda wiggled the devil horns, which looked right at home in her unruly locks, and Dez hesitated awkwardly before walking into the entryway.

Speaking of the devil, Yolanda's 4-year-old ran up behind his mom. He was little for his age. Dez judged against memories of her niece at this age. He was cute and missing a front tooth like a jack-o-lantern. He immediately became Mr. O'Lantern in her head.

"Hello, sir," she bowed to Michael, who giggled.

He tugged at his mom's shirt and whispered, "I can't find him."

"Daddy is so good at hiding!" Yolanda smiled. She looked back at Dez and shook her head. "It's almost as if he's not home at all, like he's just vanished or gone somewhere he's not supposed to go."

Dez stared blankly, having no idea how a human responds to such words.

"Maybe if we watch a video, he'll get tired of hiding and come out," Yolanda suggested. She walked Michael toward the big glass table, dialed something up on a tablet, and slid it across to the child, who sat obediently to watch. Then she shuffled Dez back toward the kitchen and put the devil horns on Dez's head.

"We could also just break Daddy's legs to make it harder for him to escape," she whispered. "Or easier to catch, with the limp and all."

Dez smiled and shook her head, hoping that was the correct way to react.

"When are you and Howie going to hook up?" Yolanda asked her. "Somebody should have a little romance, right?"

Dez considered mentioning lunch, but the cat ran past them through the kitchen, and she lost her focus.

"What do you think of Joshua Brose?" Yolanda asked, smiling coyly.

Dez didn't really understand the question. She hadn't ever thought about Joshua Brose specifically. Dez instinctively mistrusted and avoided authority figures, and since Joshua Brose ran the theater and the film festival, that was his category. Plus, he was a ginger. She tried to do as asked and generate an opinion, though. She pictured him with his perfectly coiffed red hair and pointy red beard, vests with shining threads. She thought he looked like a magician, so she said so. Yolanda took it in stride.

"I like men who look like they could be magicians," she said. "I could watch men in leather pants all day. Hey, are you going to the hospital to see Grant?"

Yolanda's question made Dez wince.

"I'm not that great in person," she said, bending to pet the cat. Yolanda stared at her, not responding. It felt like a very mom thing to do, which made Dez feel obligated to explain. "Whenever I go to a hospital, I'm afraid they won't let me back out."

"You're a coward," Yolanda told her, opening a bag of candy. She poured the contents into a big plastic pumpkin. She tossed a couple pieces at Dez, took a bite of a Fun Size Butterfinger, and continued. "We should go so his family knows we support him and believe he didn't do it."

Unwrapping her piece, Dez responded without thinking, "He clearly did it."

"Yeah," Yolanda fit a second entire Fun Size Butterfinger in with the unfinished first. "Oh, he definitely did it. He broke into a house with an ax, all Jack Nicholson-like."

Dez stopped. "Why would he do that?"

Yolanda continued to busy herself, pouring candy and tossing empty plastic bags. She held up her hands to signal, *who knows?*

Michael ran in, his hands out for candy. Yolanda smiled, put one piece in each little hand, closed the fingers around each treat, and kissed his head. Delighted, he ran back to the living room couch and his video. Yolanda's gaze stayed with her boy, but Dez — who felt like she'd been waiting to ask for a long time — broke the spell.

"Have you watched it yet?"

"Watched what?"

Dez stomped impatiently. "The *Grant* movie!"

Yolanda waved her off.

"Just watch it. Seriously. It's weirdly connected."

Yolanda caught Dez's eyes. She leaned across the wrapper-cluttered counter, put her hands over Dez's, and said, "You're trying to creep me out."

Dez shook her hands loose, and Yolanda laughed. She picked up the pumpkin of candy and headed toward the front door, asking over her shoulder, "You want to stick around for the festivities?"

Sensing the approach of excitement, Michael abandoned his video and ran back into the room.

"Can I wear it all day?!" Michael pleaded.

"Ship's ahoy, big daddy! Let's get your pirate on."

Michael jumped around like he was on a pogo stick, and Dez realized the conversation was over. He looked very cute, though. He made her giggle.

"I better get," she said. "You guys have a fun night, though, OK?"

Airborne, Michael promised, "OK!"

"You start taking off your shoes and sweater," Yolanda told him. "Leave the rest on. I'll be right back, and we'll get you ready."

Michael went from midair to a squat and started wiggling out of his light-up shoes.

Yolanda piled his costume, pointed hat on top, on the floor in front of her son, and then handed the bag to Dez.

"I got you a little something for keeping Church," she told her. "Your house needs some kind of decor, man."

While Yolanda walked Dez to the porch, she checked over her shoulder to see that Michael was out of earshot.

"Have you seen that fan video about Grant and Adam?" she asked Dez quietly, pulling her phone from her back pocket. "They're all like, 'Look how cool this horror fest is. People die and shit.'"

That seemed…what did that seem? Dez knew there was a word for it, but that word was not inventive.

"I guess ticket sales are suddenly up, though," Yolanda added cynically. "At least there's that. I can't believe we're still going through with it."

Yolanda brought the video up on her phone and handed it to Dez, saying, "His camerawork sucks, but that ink is even worse."

Yolanda's phone was sticky. Of course, she had a 4-year-old, and everything she owned was sticky. The video on the small screen was a little blurry and bouncy, but it looked like someone was running across a street toward the MacGuffin theater. Suddenly, the face of a heavily tattooed man with long hair filled the screen. He stopped running, held the phone a little further out in front of him so you could see the theater behind, and said, "This is the place! It's like a ghost tour but metal!"

Dez whispered to an inattentive Yolanda, "Does he look like someone?"

Tattoos pointed to the theater behind him. It was a modern building, built during an urban renewal period maybe fifteen years before. Tattoos stood near the high wall that overshadowed a big, empty parking lot. He put his face right in the camera.

"This is the spot for the Mayhem and Madness Film Festival."

The image jostled.

"Oh, just another horror fest, right? Maybe not! Because this fest might be the death of you!"

The shaky cam effect was never Dez's favorite. *The Blair Witch Project* was worth it, but she wasn't sure about this video as she started to feel headachy, the image bouncing as Tattoos darted around in front of the building.

"Earlier this week, one of the fest's judges gutted his wife like a fish before plunging that same bloody knife into his own throat!" Tattoos made devil fingers in excitement.

Dez could just make out Joshua Brose—probably arriving for work. Hard to miss, his highly styled red hair making him look like a lit match in a boldly patterned suit. He glanced at Tattoos with passing interest before heading into the theater.

"Yeah!" Tattoos hooped. "Real horror show! But that's not all! Another judge broke into his childhood home with an ax and some gasoline! As he was swinging away with the ax, a neighbor shot him point blank!"

Tattoos got quiet, talking directly into his camera.

"Will it end there? Or will somebody else go off his rocker and on a killing spree? Maybe it'll even happen at the festival! Well, I, for one, will be there to find out!" He suddenly burst with energy. "MAYHEM!!!"

Again, with the devil fingers.

CHAPTER FOUR

She saw a text from Howie when she closed the driver-side door—a link to the same video Yolanda showed her with the message: *did you see this?!*

She texted back: *too nutty!*

That seemed normal, right? Or was it too flippant? Did it not reflect a proper level of horror when facing murdered and murdering friends? What is the normal level? Her thoughts were interrupted when the phone rang. It rang! Startled, she tossed it into the backseat and then had to retrieve it before it stopped ringing.

"Hello, hey, hi, hey," she stuttered.

"Did you hear about the stash?" Howie asked.

OK, so that was an even weirder opening. "Stash of?"

"So, I guess there were like...well...

inappropriate photos in the floor where Grant was chopping."

"Like porn?"

"I guess it was worse than that," he paused. Was he embarrassed? Was he worried he would offend her?

"They didn't mention that on the news," she answered.

"Maybe they're keeping it quiet while they investigate," Howie thought.

"How did you find out?"

"I was talking with Joshua. He says the pictures might be of Grant and his sister, who killed herself back in high school, I guess?"

"Why were you talking to Joshua?"

Why was everybody always talking to Joshua?

"He just called to see how I was bearing up with all the mishaps," Howie told her.

Huh. Dez made a mental note not to answer if Joshua called, having no idea on planet Earth how to respond to that question.

She wanted to tell Howie and Yolanda to stop talking to him. You can never trust a ginger — didn't they know that?

"Anyway, I knew you were curious and thought I'd share the intel."

She smiled. She wanted him to laugh. Howie had such a great laugh. But this was probably the wrong time, dead people and all. Right? She couldn't think of anything funny to say, anyway, and then suddenly realized she'd been entirely quiet for like maybe a really long time.

"You OK?"

"I am!" she said, way, way too loudly and happily.

He laughed.

"Glad to hear it. Lester says hey!"

"Hey to Lester."

"We should get Mexican again."

"Today?"

He laughed again. He didn't mean today, of course. Only Dez eats Chipotle twice in the same day.

"Maybe not today. I have weird shifts

the next couple of days, but I'll text you."

"Sure!" Again, if only she could dial down the excitement.

"Cool."

***

Cool. Dez was still thinking about it when she reached home, absently wearing Yolanda's devil horns and dropping her keys and Yolanda's shopping bag on her kitchen counter. She fished a picture frame from the bag and pulled a pile of photos out of a drawer near the sink. Carrying the whole mess toward the table, she avoided eye contact with her laptop.

She found a photo of herself, her sister, and a little girl. Dez's wrists were still in bandages, but she loved this picture anyway. Two years ago, so Maude would've been about 6 in this shot. The three were at Cedar Point, and there was a colorful and wildly expensive little snack hut behind them, the blue Agave Grove sign the same color as Maude's eyes. The three were hugging each other in the shot. The height difference made them look a bit like two little lemurs happily hanging from the tree that was Dez. It was Dez's favorite photo ever.

She set it on the top of the closed laptop and began to peel the price sticker from the glass of the frame, wondering if she'd need a butter knife to get it off, when the lure of the laptop became too much. She slid the photo and frame to the table, lifted the silver lid, and found Tattoo's viral video.

"Where will it end?"

She paused the video, opened the tab with the film festival portal, and hovered over the link to the short film *Grant* a few seconds before clicking. She figured she might just watch it again for clues.

She didn't want to see what was in the floor, but she really wanted to see what was in the floor. No way it was a coincidence that this movie had a stash of photos in the floor of the exact same house where Grant tried to break through the floor with an ax. Right? How was that a coincidence?

She looked. She paused at the stash in

the floor. She squinted and tried to expand the image with her fingers, which was stupid because it was a laptop. Duh.

"What is that?"

She stared, but she couldn't make anything out. It could have been a stack of old photos, sure. But it could just as easily have been movie props, like the set designer's family portraits piled on top of stuff mined from a thrift shop or something.

"If this was a movie, I'd somehow break into an evidence room at a police station," Dez said. She often talked to herself at home and was so rarely not at home that she worried she might actually do it all day, every day. She probably needed a pet.

"I'd wade through those pictures and revisit all the evidence. With the help of a hot policeman," her fantasy continued. "Who'd die violently before we ever got to have sex."

She texted Yolanda: *I'm Naomi Watts in The Ring*

Yolanda texted back: *You're Brian Cox*

"What?!"

Annoyed, Dez removed the horns and called Yolanda.

"In what way am I Brian Cox?"

"You're scary, and you have a little bit of acne scarring on your cheek," Yolanda told her.

"Fuck you," she laughed. "I mean, I'm Naomi Watts because I'm sleuthing out the connection between this short film and our hospitalized friend."

***

"Oh, he's your friend now?"

Yolanda stood in her kitchen, phone pinched between shoulder and ear, readjusting Michael's eye patch. She wasn't sure she really needed this at the moment. She handed Michael his three-pointed hat and smiled at how cute he looked, his one good eye full of joy, the hole in his smile making this pirate that much sweeter.

"Have you watched it yet?" Dez was asking.

"*The Ring*?" Yolanda pretended not

to know what she meant because life was easier sometimes if people just expected you to be flighty. "You know I'm more of a *Ringu* girl."

"*Grant*." There was a touch of annoyance, maybe desperation, in Dez's voice.

Yolanda turned Michael around and looked him over. God damn, this kid was cute. Good-looking like his daddy but with a loyal, kind heart and a silly personality. Like Yolanda. She smiled, gave him a thumbs up, and hoped to find a polite way to end this phone call.

"No," she admitted. "I have not watched it."

"Why not?"

"It's morbid."

She could feel Dez lose steam. This new, clingy Dez was more of a strain than Yolanda needed. Mark was enough of a strain. Day in, day out, disappointment and strain. And Joshua—now he was a strain, too. Deciding what to do about this pregnancy when she hadn't had sex with her husband in almost a year — strain strain strain. People dying and getting shot all over the damn place, strain! Yolanda wanted to have something left for Dez, but she didn't. She just did not.

"They're all morbid," Dez countered. "That's the point."

"You're making this one too morbid."

Yolanda needed to get her coat if she wanted to avoid conflict. You'd think this woman would have some respect for trick-or-treat, the holiest of family nights! She could hear Michael tugging the husband, who decided to grace them with his presence, toward the front door.

"Where is Grant's dad? Dead, right?" Dez asked her.

Yolanda looked at her boys, quietly responding, "I don't know."

Dez pushed on. "And his mom is dead?"

"I have no idea," Yolanda told her, impatience growing.

She grabbed warm fleeces from the hall closet, handed a plastic bag for candy overflow to her husband, and ushered the family through the door and toward the growing throng of ghouls outside. She should have hung up right then. That's what she should have done.

"Is this guy in the movie his real dad or a stepdad or something?"

That was it. Yolanda just wanted a nice, spooky night with her sweet boy and the husband, who was, at least right now, playing along. She set her feet and said, "Neither. The guy in the movie is an actor. That is how movies work."

The pause on the other end made Yolanda feel a little guilty. She pushed the boys out into the night, held up a "just a minute finger" toward her husband, and softened toward Dez.

"I'm sorry, yeah?" she said. "Joshua told me Grant was not close with his family."

"Why are you always talking with Joshua Brose?" Yolanda felt a little accusation in the question.

"Why does that matter? Do you want to hear this or not? Joshua says Grant actually hated that he had to drive past that house to get to the theater for the festival every year. I don't know about his mom, but he hated his dad. It caused some kind of riff with his sister, Elise, who I guess sided with the dad. Grant even took his mom's last name as an adult. His dad's name was Horrocks. Donovan Horrocks—that's a mouthful." She paused for a second. "I'm going now."

***

Dez sat dazed and staring in the bland white of her dining room, still holding her phone to her face.

"Horrocks," she murmured. "Elise Horrocks."

Her doorbell startled her back to reality.

Is Tamara home?
You are gonna die in there!
Ding dong. You're dead.
Brian Cox opened that door in *Trick*

'r Treat.

She pushed horror movie taglines and images out of her head and snuck through the growing shadows of the house toward the front door to peek through the high window. A very smiley little freckled face greeted her.

Dez chuckled, relieved, and opened up.

Grace and her daughter gathered on the little concrete porch. Grace was struggling to hold Maude up to the high window, and she let her drop to her feet as Dez opened the door. It struck Dez how different Maude already looked from the photo she loved. She was taller, her face a little thinner, and Grace — well, Grace was much plumper now, but pregnancy will do that.

Maude struck a pose in her Halloween costume. She looked like she had a giant, homemade octopus around her neck. Dez was lost. Lost but happy.

"Hello!!" she cheered, hugging her

niece with glee. A stray octopus arm tangled in her hair.

"Hey!" Grace said. "I know you hate unannounced visits like you hate unannounced raisins, but I thought you'd want to see Maude in her costume."

"Unannounced raisins are so disappointing," Dez admitted.

"Because you think they're chocolate chips!" Maude agreed.

"Right?!!" Dez stepped onto the crowded little porch to better examine the costume. "You look amazing. Incredible Hulk, right?"

Maude giggled. She said, as much to her mother as to her aunt, "There are kids in costumes at a park we passed. Do you think they're giving out candy? Can we go see?"

"Surely!" Dez had a taste for candy as well.

The trio turned merrily away from Dez's front door and piled into Grace's big mom car. Over its roof, Dez asked her sister, "Hey, do you remember Elise Horrocks?"

Grace responded, "What a hideous name! No. I don't know her."

Dez nodded, got into the passenger seat, and buckled herself in. The car smelled like gingerbread — it always smelled like gingerbread, and laughter from the backseat sounded like bells. As much as she hated cars, Dez was almost always happy in this vehicle. But today, she sat quiet and preoccupied until everyone else burst out of the minivan and into the park.

***

As Maude sped toward throngs of other costumed youngsters, Dez broached the subject again.

"She was Colleen Kierney's best friend."

Grace flinched at the name, then asked, "Who was?"

"Elise Horrocks."

Dez and Grace walked in silence for a minute, following the wake Maude made. The grass of the park was still greenish, with four little playgrounds distributed throughout, each guarded by one large tree shooting up like a mangled hand reaching for God. Kids in costumes scattered about the park, many pooling around booths set up with games. Grace and Dez eyed these as they walked past, looking for a bobbing octopus.

"What's up with Elise Horrocks these days?" Grace inquired, her tone light.

"She's dead," Dez told her, then reconsidered. "I think."

"Oh." Grace's tone was artificially nonchalant as she waddled a little slowly and pretended to check out everyone's costumes. They caught up with Maude, who was taking a turn at a fish tank game.

"Like, dead for a long time, maybe," Dez continued. "It's secondhand intel, but I'm pretty sure she's dead. Maybe."

Grace looked at her sister, confused and maybe alarmed. Dez pushed on.

"I didn't realize it, but Elise Horrocks's brother is Grant, another festival judge."

"OK," Grace gently took Dez's arm

and led her away from the kids and the fish game just as Maude snagged a cheap plastic figure with a colorful parachute. She wasn't sure where this was going, but she was sure it was going nowhere good.

"This is the guy who killed his wife?" Grace asked.

"No. The other one."

"Ax guy?"

"Yes."

Grace held up her hand, signaling Dez to stop talking while Maude ran toward her mom and aunt to show off her prize. Dez and Grace clapped excitedly as Maude tossed the creature into the air and then ran off to follow its trajectory on the wind.

Dez continued.

"So, there was this short film online the other day called *Adam*."

"That's the name of the first guy?" Grace stopped to clarify. "Who killed his wife?"

"Yeah, Adam Vivod. Super nice, always smiling, could never bring himself to say something bad about a movie because he sincerely rooted for everybody who'd worked on it," she said. Her speech got faster and faster as she talked.

They stopped following Maude and took side-by-side seats on a swing set. It reminded Grace of being a kid on the creaky blue and white swings their dad put in in the back yard without sinking the legs. If they swung high enough, they could get the front legs to come six inches off the ground.

"Adam seemed like the nicest man in the world," Dez said. "And then he just murdered his wife the day after that movie called *Adam* showed up. And then, and then, after that, when I went to find the movie *Adam* online, it wasn't in the queue anymore! It had disappeared!"

Grace studied her sister. It was quiet for a beat, Dez looking expectantly toward her.

"Spooky," Grace said in her best Halloween voice.

Dez got excited. "Right? *Adam* wasn't

there, but instead, there was a movie called *Grant*."

Grace stopped moving the swing. She turned an almost laughing look on her sister.

"The name of the guy with the ax?"

Dez nodded. "So, I watched that one."

"Naturally," was Grace's wry response. Her eyes moved from her sister to her daughter, who was ambling in their direction. Dez's eyes followed.

"They're not giving out treats," Maude reported. "Just pencils."

"Lame!" Grace declared.

Maude's face turned to exaggerated anxiety. "We should get home before trick-or-treat, right?"

Dez laughed, Grace wondered what happened to the parachuter, and they all headed back to the minivan. Dez's phone binged repeatedly, but she ignored it.

"Yolanda," she explained. "She never texts just once. It's always a machine gun thing with her."

Grace pulled over in front of her

sister's house but made no move to turn off the car. As Dez got out, she lowered her face to the passenger window to peer in at Grace. She threw her head in a *come out here a minute* way.

Grace sighed and put the car in park. She stepped out but didn't close her door, looking again at her sister over the roof.

"The movie *Grant* is definitely filmed at the house my friend Grant broke into."

"With an ax," Grace replied.

"Yes."

Grace looked at her sister with understanding and just a hint of mockery, as was her way.

"So, you think these movies are cursed?" she inquired. "Like *The Ring*."

"Shut up."

Grace made spooky hands and whispered in that Halloween voice, "Seven days..."

Maude rolled down the window to look out. Dez told her, "Your mom's going to eat all your good candy as soon as you go to bed."

"No!!!" Maude shouted.

Grace giggled, "It's a family tradition!" and walked around the car to hug her sister. "Don't watch any more scary movies today."

Dez ignored her. She peeked her head in Maude's car window with a request: "Save me some candy."

Maude waved her off nonchalantly. "No way, lady."

"Quit this festival," Grace said, taking Dez's arm. "Seriously. You were doing better, and now it feels all bad vibey again. And apparently, these movies kill people, and who needs that?"

Dez nodded, but her sister wasn't buying.

"Just quit. Right? Once you start thinking your life is a horror movie—right? Just gotta keep a grip on reality this time."

She threw the conversation to her daughter, still peering out the window.

"Right, chica? No more crazy for Auntie Destiny?"

Maude gave Dez a thumbs-up.

"Quit."

"Yeah, quit!" Maude parroted.

"I will," Dez promised.

CHAPTER FIVE

Grace waddled back to the driver's side. As Dez waved at the departing vehicle, her phone buzzed again. She took in a deep, cleansing breath and made a sort of elephant noise as she blew it out. It wasn't until she was inside the house that she mustered interest in Yolanda's texts.

She only read one: *Grant died*
"Jesus Christ."

She sat right where she was, her front door behind her, her open coat closet in front of her, and Googled "Grant Arbogast" on her phone. She scrolled through a number of options:

Film Festival attacker dies in hospital

Horror movie maker facing charges dies of gunshot wound

Another Mayhem Fest Killer Bites It!!!

Yep, that last one was the one. Dez

clicked to find another video from the same tattooed man she had seen earlier. She braced for the shaky cam and ghoulish take on the situation as soon as she saw the big, open porch. Tattoos was standing outside the house Dez saw in the film called *Grant*.

"Dudes!" he yelled into his phone's camera, then he turned solemn. "It has happened. The second judge associated with Murder and Mayhem film fest died today."

Tattoos spun the phone and swept the scene, picking up the sagging police tape still littering the lawn as he narrated.

"Grant Arbogast broke into this house with an ax and a gallon of gasoline, got shot by neighbors, and is now dead in the hospital."

His grin was wicked when he turned the camera back on himself.

"Don't forget ol' Adam Vivod. You remember the fest judge who gutted his woman then tore his own throat out?!"

He jumped up and down with excitement, the camera flying this way and that, Dez's stomach lurching with it. He was evangelizing again even before the image focused.

"It's horror, man! You're either in, or you're out. I need to find out: Who's next?!" He brought the camera in for an extreme close-up. "Is it you?!"

Does life imitate art, or does art imitate life? Dez couldn't remember. Maybe art recreates life—that seemed correct but not poetic enough to be right.

Dez looked back at the screen, back at Tattoos.

"Who is that guy?"

She squinted, replayed the video, and watched closely.

"Is it you?!"

She cocked her head as the camera came in close.

Dez walked to her laptop in the dining room to bring the video up on a larger screen.

"Is it you?!" he said again.

She opened another tab and dug around until she found the fest marketing partner Killer Pictures website. She clicked about and landed on the guy with the man bun. No tattoos, no close-up. Still...

"Is that you?" she asked him.

She clicked the video again.

"Is it you?!"

There was a resemblance. Maybe. Maybe not. She closed her laptop, tired of herself. But she had to admit, "That would be one way to get people to the festival. Of course, you'd go to hell for doing it."

A thought smacked her, and she flipped the laptop open again. She brought up the site with the festival queue and scrolled.

Meatboat

Does Lauren Look Hungry?

Obstacle Corpse

No *Grant* movie.

"You are fucking kidding me."

She hesitated for about a second before calling Grace. It rang and rang, and Dez wondered what exactly she'd say in a message when Grace finally picked up. She could tell by the racket that her sister was outside, then she remembered it was Trick-or-Treat.

***

Costumed children spilled off suburban porches: skeletons and baseball players, a Viking, and some clowns.

"You're missing the excitement," Grace told Dez.

The inflatable dinosaur suits made Grace giggle, and she made a mental note for next year. She watched Maude rush toward a throng of superheroes. Grace smiled but struggled to keep up.

"Grant—the ax guy—just died," Dez said soberly. "And his movie disappeared from the site."

"What?" Grace slowed. She watched the octopus head bob up a walkway and toward a front porch light.

"The movie disappeared as soon as Grant Arbogast died," Dez clarified. In her voice, Grace heard strangled panic. She chose to keep it light.

"No. Way!"

"I swear to God."

"I feel like you need a microfiche machine," Grace said, a patient, even affectionate smile working its way into her voice. "And like a big library, old newsprint, and you'll find somebody in an asylum somewhere who will help you unravel a curse."

"Shut up," Dez told her.

"You're sleuthing out clues to put an end to the horror movie you're living," Grace pointed out.

"I know!"

"I'm making fun of you," Grace said.

"Oh." She could hear Dez deflate. "I'm imagining things."

"Oh, definitely," Grace confirmed. "How fun!"

Grace looked around at little pods of fake fur, plastic capes, and Disney princesses and wished this reality for her sister.

"Hey, what if we looked into art therapy?" Grace suddenly thought. "Instead of watching movies all the time, alone and in your head, you could make movies. Or write books or make art or something?"

"I took Elise Horrocks to the party."

Grace stopped walking. A little Spider-Man bumped right into her, the stop was so abrupt.

"What?"

Dez didn't answer right away but eventually repeated, "Elise Horrocks. I took her to the party."

"*The* party?" Grace needed confirmation.

"*The* party," Dez confirmed.

Grace shook her head around to sort the message and resumed walking. She wasn't certain where Maude was, but she moved with the wave to the next house.

"You didn't leave the party with her. Obviously."

"No," Dez sounded — not sad, exactly, not guilty, exactly — resigned.

"What happened?"

***

"Colleen wanted to bring her," Dez remembered. She'd hardly even remembered that Elise Horocks had been there, honestly. It had never come up since the accident that Dez could recall. Elise probably wasn't supposed to be at the party—really, none of them were supposed to be there, sophomores at Jason Dietz's graduation bash. Of course, Grace wouldn't remember her there, she was in the 8th grade and spared of it until the ambulance, thank God.

But Elise Horrocks had definitely come in Dez's car. She remembered that now. She had on this ugly pea-colored dress. And then Dez couldn't really recall anything until the beer pong, but they'd already had so much to drink in the car. Then Colleen retched. Dez shepherded Colleen and Jenny Beans back to the car, flagged down Angie Comer, who jumped into the backseat with Jenny, and they drove off.

"I had forgotten she was even with us," Dez told her sister. "Things got nutty, and you know the rest."

"You left without her," Grace said. Dez could tell she wasn't walking anymore; she couldn't hear the labored breathing. She knew Grace was devoting all her attention to the story now. "Destiny, I hate to be a dick about this, but you did her a favor leaving her behind. You know that."

Dez stared absently at the growing shadow in the corner of the room.

"I never even spoke to her again," she whispered into the phone.

"Or she never spoke to you again, Dez," she heard her sister say. Dez was cold. Was she cold? She wanted a blanket. Or a dog. Or Maude. Something warm.

"I mean, a lot of people never spoke to you again after the accident." It was just a statement of fact, the kind of thing Grace would say to keep Destiny grounded. "Which just means Elise Horrocks was as big an asshole as everyone else."

Dez frowned.

"Don't relive it," Grace broke in just as Dez began to float back to that night.

"Remember what Dr. Bonen said."

"Stop having sex with nurse aides? You got a good kid fired today?"

"No. But don't relive that, either. No, she said that people relive trauma to try to control it and change the outcome. But you just wind up spending all your time inside the very worst moments of your life because you can't change the outcome."

"Five nice people died because of me. They didn't deserve to die."

"Neither do you," Grace told her. "It haunts you, so you look for a new, tidier ending, like a movie. Something to wrap it up so it can be over." Grace breathed deep. Braced herself. "Destiny, it's never really going to be over. But you can move on."

***

It was too loud out. The wind was picking up, and a house nearby had creaky, clangy, spooky music playing from a porch speaker. Grace wanted to be able to hear Destiny breathing. It would help her know how her anxiety was. Still, she had to be clear. No soft gloves this time. That made everything worse the last time.

"It was so much like a horror movie," her sister moaned.

"No, it wasn't, actually," Grace said. "High school kids got too drunk to realize they shouldn't be driving. That's a tragedy, Destiny, but a pretty common one. And you need to stop reliving it."

Grace waited for an answer and realized she wasn't breathing.

"It's the only thing I've ever really done, though."

Flabbergasted, Grace lost her train of thought, and then she recovered.

"So now your movie plot is that this Horrocks girl has returned from the grave to seek bloody revenge?" A thought dawned on Grace. "Wait, what makes us even think she's dead?"

Good God, she couldn't even see Maude. Grace started rushing through neighbors and strangers, peeking onto porches. She couldn't even tell if her sister had responded to the question.

"She's probably fine, Destiny," Grace told her. "There's something narcissistic about believing you are responsible for everything."

Grace stopped moving and looked around. Maude was nowhere. She closed her eyes, her face turning ugly.

"I'm sorry she wasn't in the fucking car. If she was dead in the car exactly like everybody else, you wouldn't be able to relive the fucking accident right now."

Maude tugged on the back of Grace's coat. Relieved, she turned and nodded at her daughter, who was obviously annoyed she was on the phone again. She was so happy to see her daughter she barely heard her sister whisper.

"Like she was meant to be in the car?"

"What?" Grace asked.

"Like a sequel?" her sister whispered back.

"What?! No!" She stomped her foot. "There is no movie plot, no narrative. There's no playback here, OK? You have survivor's guilt. Still. Obviously. But you did this girl a favor by leaving her at the party."

Grace's voice sounded impatient. She hated the way she sounded. She made an effort to sound cheerier. "Meet us back at our house. You can help me steal all Maude's candy."

"No." Dez's voice was defiant.

"Do we need to come there?"

Dez said more softly, "No."

"Are you sure?"

"Yes."

Grace softened as tenderness returned to her sister's voice.

"Do not watch any more scary movies!" Grace commanded. "Stop torturing yourself. And stop looking stuff up about your dead friends."

Dez protested weakly. "They're not like friend friends."

"That's right," Grace said with that voice that sounded like a teacher or a therapist. Or a mom. She sounded rehearsed, talking in a measured, soothing tone. "Who are your friend friends?"

Dez replied, sounding a bit like a child.

"Yolanda is my friend. And Michael. Her son. Michael is my friend. Mr. O'Lantern."

"You're right," Grace agreed. "And Yolanda's fine, right? And Michael's fine. Nothing has happened to them."

"Right."

"And you're fine."

"Yes."

"Are you sure you won't meet us at my house?"

"No."

Grace paused, then suggested in a calm and measured tone, "Dez, you need to come to our house. Or we need to come to yours. I don't like you alone right now."

"What about a friend? I could have a friend over."

Grace contemplated. "Promise?"

She heard her sister take a deep breath

and exhale slowly.
      "Yep."

CHAPTER SIX

Dez hung up and rubbed her eyes. She looked at her laptop. She lingered, suspicious. She lifted the lid. She closed it again.

Own it. There was nothing supernatural, no curse, no evil.

How should she own it but not relive it? She thought that was how she was supposed to own it. Don't shut it out. Accept it. Acknowledge the pain. Although, did she still feel pain? Did she ever? Yes, she must have. But before pain, it was the sound, the dry gravel sound under her wheels, that made her think of trips to Toledo with her dad. And the spotlight effect of her headlights on the dirty road ahead of her. And the air, because the windows were open since Jenny Beans had puked in the back seat. And she knew her brain could fill in that next big blank—what happened? what did she hit?

how did she hit it?—but it wouldn't be a memory. It would be fiction, dramatization because the next memory was later. After the screams, because there must have been screams. After the blood, the horrific sound of the crash, the sight of a body she knew launched through the windshield, and of a body she did not know launching toward her from across the hood.

She was aware of all that must have happened, but what she saw in her head was just her brain's own movie of it. So, it changed most times, sometimes with quick edits, sometimes in slow motion. Sometimes jump scares, sometimes classic dread. It never really matched with the dry realism of the rest of her biopic horror show, though, and what came after.

She saw it again, a freeze frame like a painting, exactly as she saw it while they wheeled her toward the gaping rear of the ambulance. Blood drizzled and trickled down the hood of one car, pooling on the crumpled bumper of the other before drip,

drip, dripping on the street and making a little stream in the asphalt toward Angie Comer's pointing finger.

Stop reliving it.

She didn't really know how to do that.

Have a friend over.

She knew how to do that. She wasn't very much better at it than she was at figuring out how to own something without reliving it, but rather than dwell on Angie Comer's finger, she could dwell on Howie's lovely crooked bottom teeth.

She texted Howie: *Do you want to come to my house?*

About an hour later, Dez and Howie were making out in her kitchen while Lester contentedly gnawed a bone from Grace's leftovers.

Dez and Howie were awkward but sweet, two half-drunk beer bottles on the counter behind them. Howie was very warm. His lips were full and soft, and she wanted to bite them. His torso was so lean, and she couldn't help but slide her hand under his Halloween III tee shirt to see how velvety it was. Oh, so very velvety.

He made her think of that nurse's aide who smelled so nice, blotting out the antiseptic odor of her hospital room when he stood close to her to gently check her gauze or dump the pills out of the little white cup right into her palm. The warmest smile and that snaggletooth! Crooked teeth—her Achilles heel! He'd gotten fired, though, hadn't he, because of it? Because of her? Was this like that? Was this also bad? This is why she keeps herself far away from human bodies, isn't it? She had such a hard time knowing.

Howie stopped for a second, his face hovering close to hers.

"Right. Right," she smiled, dreamily aware that she didn't really know what to do. Was he ready to leave? He should leave, right? Is this the point where they part? This is nice, though, isn't it? She so rarely knew what she was supposed to do, only what she wanted to do. So, she took his hand and walked back to her bedroom. Lester looked up but continued with his bone.

It was nice not thinking about movies and mysteries and dead people. It was nice not thinking. It was nice, even walking Howie to the back door, collecting Lester, and kissing goodbye.

He opened the kitchen door, and she realized his Halloween III tee shirt was inside out. Then he turned back to her, smiling, and asked, "Why are you single?"

Nope. What? Nope. My head is full of flies and wax. I'm a hollow shell. I'm a murderer.

"My only true loves are Mexican food and scary movies," she answered. Damn. That was nonsense but it bordered on coherent, even charming. Maybe. "Why are you single?"

Howie didn't seem prepared for that, which was odd because he asked first and wasn't that what she was supposed to do? Respond in kind?

He stepped back into the house,

unconsciously rubbing Lester's head.

"My last girlfriend, she had all these big ideas, you know?" He looked like he was nervous to say it out loud. "Really smart and ambitious. Fearless. And she made me feel like we could do some kind of big, crazy things together. But mainly, she just wanted me to do whatever she wanted me to do, you know? And she was mean. Not like you. You're really kind. And weird, but good weird."

She smiled. Her smile felt weird but good weird. Like Angela Bettis in *May*, when Jeremy Sisto and his beautiful hands told her he liked weird. Yes, she turned out to be too weird for him. He broke her heart, and things ended badly for him. Dez reset, tried to recapture the moment she'd just ruined. Because even May got to be happy for that one moment.

Howie smooched her forehead. "Don't watch any more movies."

"Right," she agreed. "You either."

"Yeah, right!" he said on the way

back out the door. "You got me all sucked into the mystery now." As he opened the car door for Lester and waved, he called, "Hey, I'm off work at 7. I could come get you for breakfast?"

Dez nodded happily and turned back to her house. She kept smiling, dumped the leftover beer and put the bottles in recycling. The cold of the floor crept through the soles of her feet, and she dashed back to her bedroom to find socks. She tried not to notice the laptop perched on her dining room table as she passed.

She returned, stocking-footed, and tried walking past the laptop again.

It didn't work.

"Nope, nope, nope, nope..."

She sat down. Sighed. Opened the laptop. She found the film fest site.

"I am not looking," she said to no one. She tapped the table with her fingertips. "What was Grant's dad's name?"

She clicked out of the film site and instead Googled 'Donovan Horrocks.' She chose the Wikipedia page that came up. The photo on the page was the handsome man from the *Grant* movie.

"Fuck!" she yelped. "Oh, fuck me..."

She skimmed to a string of movie credits ending in the Nineties.

"*The Black Coat*? *Lovers Lament*? How have I never even heard of these?"

She called Grace again.

"Dude, I'm on Grant's dad's Wikipedia page," she blurted the moment Grace picked up.

***

Not far away, but too far, she was beginning to realize, Grace sat at a big table sorting through pieces of candy, inspecting them, and dropping them back into Maude's Halloween bucket.

"God damn it."

Grace could tell from the tiny gasp on the line that Dez had realized her mistake in calling.

"It's fine," she heard Dez backpedal. "I'm not responsible. I'm just curious."

Grace sighed, resigned. She looked at the eager little face waiting for candy and played along with her sister. "Which one is Grant? Ax guy or wife?"

"Ax guy," Dez confirmed, sounding relieved. "And maybe Elise's brother."

"And?" Grace's impatience seeped out, even though she was trying to keep it in. She listened as Dez read from the screen.

"Donovan Horrocks had a promising career, starring in several cult films. Rumors of spousal abuse and occult activity dogged the actor, and by the early Nineties…"

"Occult activity?" Grace interrupted. This was so dumb. Who would write that?

"Right?!" she heard the excitement in her sister's voice.

Grace stood and walked the OK'd candy over to Maude. She pretended not to give her daughter the booty, relented, and handed her the loaded plastic pumpkin. Maude sat on the fluffy white area rug, and Grace realized the waiting disaster after handing her so much chocolate. Grace smiled, but the smile turned sad. She walked out of the room, away from Maude, and into her dark kitchen, still fragrant with the smell of grilled cheese and tomato soup.

"It's Wikipedia, though, right?" Grace said. "Anyone could have written that. I could go on Wikipedia right now and say he bathed every night in pudding."

"Or the blood of children," her sister replied.

"Pudding's more fun, but honestly, they would be equally hard to clean up," Grace said. "The point is that whoever made your movie could have invented the write-up for, like, viral marketing or something. Like *Blair Witch*."

"Dude, this is totally happening," Dez responded.

Grace remembered the last time — the suicide attempt, visiting hours, that poor orderly Destiny had fucked right in the hospital bed and gotten fired. She rested a hand on her ample belly and sighed.

"God, I wish you liked romantic

comedies. It would be so much easier if you kept thinking your life was a romantic comedy. Destiny, come over here," she said. "Right now. We'll drink some beer—well, you can—and we'll all watch *ParaNorman*. You like that one."

The first time they'd seen *ParaNorman*, Maude was definitely too young for it. She sat the whole time in Dez's lap, terrified. Dez had not seen the movie, but because it followed all the tropes of the horror movies she knew so well, Dez could whisper what was about to happen into Maude's ear. It gave Maude confidence and reminded her that it was all made up. Dez essentially ruined the movie for anyone within earshot, but she'd saved the day for Maude, who was brave with the secret formula and eventually loved the movie.

"You can stay here," Grace offered. "The cutie would love it."

***

Destiny was about to accept the invitation when something suddenly occurred to her. She opened the film site tab.

She saw a new film.

Yolanda

"I have to go," she blurted and hung up. Dez didn't think. She just tucked her phone into her back pocket, snatched her keys from the kitchen counter, and headed out. The sky had darkened since she'd walked Howie to her door. She hated to drive when it was dark, but she didn't even take it slow. Really, she was driving somewhat recklessly away from her house and breaking one of her sacred safety rules by calling Yolanda, who didn't answer.

"Call me as soon as you get this," she said authoritatively, not panicky, to the voicemail. "Don't text—I'm driving, but I'm heading to your house. Call me before you do anything at all."

She gripped the phone and steering wheel at the same time so she'd see it light up, which happened almost immediately.

"What's up?" Yolanda almost slurred. "You're like a stalker all of the sudden."

Destiny could hear a lot of noise in the background, people talking, and music playing.

"Where are you?" she asked.

"Just needed to get out for a minute, you know?" Yolanda sounded weary and definitely a little drunk.

"There's a new movie called *Yolanda*."

Dez held her breath.

"Hang on," Yolanda said, but it sounded like she was a mile away from the phone. It got quiet, and Dez realized Yolanda had walked outside. She heard her light a cigarette and take a drag. Dez had never known Yolanda to smoke. Maybe that was how the movie would get her! Someone would spill a drink on her, her hair would catch fire, and she'd go right up!

"I can hear now," Yolanda told her.

Dez tried desperately to calm herself.

"The film *Grant* is gone, but there's a new film on the site called *Yolanda*." The calm, authoritative tone had been leached away by panic. Yolanda didn't say anything.

Why didn't Yolanda say anything? "Don't watch it," Destiny commanded.

"Are you kidding?" was the response. Was Yolanda chuckling? Angry? Terrified? Dez couldn't tell. "No, seriously," she doubled down. "Don't."

Now, Yolanda laughed. "Still with that *Ring* thing?"

This street didn't look right to Dez. She'd only driven to Yolanda's in the daytime before, and nothing looked familiar now.

"What?" She really wasn't sure what Yolanda had said. "No."

Dez signaled, pulled to the side of the road, and parked. She needed to focus.

"I'm not being funny," Dez told her friend. "Don't watch it. I think you'll die. Or kill somebody. Or both."

"Well, I might kill Mark whether I watch or not," Dez heard, frustrated that Yolanda was making light of this. "I don't need much of a push, if you know what I mean."

"I'm not kidding, though."

"Stop it," Yolanda said, no longer sounding light. "You're seriously freaking me out right now."

Dez was actually glad to have her attention. "Don't watch it."

Yolanda stayed quiet again, quiet for too long. Too, too long. Dez began to panic. "You're going to watch it, aren't you? Don't watch it. Please don't watch it."

***

Yolanda wasn't going to go back in the bar. What was the point? Joshua obviously wasn't showing up. Back of a darkened theater was fine, but out in public was a problem? It almost made her just want to stick it out with Mark, but if this baby came out with red hair...

Whatever. Meeting with Joshua this close to home would have been flatly idiotic anyway, and Yolanda knew it. Even if she had given up on Mark and the marriage — and she had, let's be honest — it was gross to flaunt this Joshua thing — whatever it was —

right here in their own neighborhood.

Yolanda decided to leave the car where it was. Her house was only a couple blocks up the road. The weather was cool but refreshing, the stars were out, and it smelled like leaves. It smelled like fall. It was a nice end to the Halloween season. Hey! What's better on Halloween than a scary movie named after you? Maybe she'd watch it for a laugh. It was only a short, so under half an hour.

No. Probably not. She felt spooked just thinking about it, so she quickened her pace, looking for the big inflatable Jack Skellington in the distance that would mean she was close to home, and came up with an idea.

"You watch it and tell me what happens."

"Now?" Dez sounded reluctant.

"Yeah, why not?" Yolanda decided. "I'll just listen."

"I don't care for this plan," Dez said. "This seems like a bad plan, like trying to trick the devil or the curse. When does that ever go well? What if it kills you anyway?"

"Destiny..." Yolanda was losing patience and interest.

"What if it's a movie of you listening to a movie over my phone only in the movie, I'm a monster, or Mark's in my bed or something, and you go crazy, come over to my house later, and kill me?"

Yolanda felt suddenly sober. Abruptly, she stopped walking. "Why would you say that? About Mark? Has Mark been over?"

"What are you even talking about?!" Dez yelled into her ear. "Of course not!!"

A little too passionate, maybe? A little too defensive?

"So, watch it," Yolanda dared her.

"No!!"

Dez's response was so loud that Yolanda kind of balked. She could see her house now, its upstairs windows glowing like eyes. Michael must be getting into bed right now. She wondered if it would even occur to Mark to read him one of his cute little monster books. No, Mark only cared about Christmas. If she hurried, Yolanda bet she could get in there before Michael was asleep and remedy that situation. And get her mind off this one.

"All right," she told Dez. "I gotta go."

She could hear Destiny's final desperate "Don't watch it!" as she hung up.

***

Dez smacked her face repeatedly against her steering wheel.

"Aaaaahhhgghghghg!!"

She collected herself. She stared ahead at a long stripe of reflection down the front of her hood from the streetlight. She breathed. Good, she checked her phone. The film *Yolanda* was still in the queue. She looked over her shoulder and pulled into the street.

Dez had definitely passed the street she needed, so she sucked it up and got on the highway. She focused on breathing in, out, in, out, in, out and looked for the German Village exits. In, out, in, out, blinker, veer, in, out, in, out. The whole fiasco probably cost her twenty minutes, but she was back on track and recognized the neighborhood.

Dez pulled over in front of Yolanda's house, put the car in park, and checked her phone, relieved to find the title *Yolanda* still on the site. She turned her attention to the house. The inflatables were now inflated, but the house behind them was dark. Dez got nervous. Even the front porch light was out, but she reminded herself that might be a choice meant to discourage late trick-or-treaters.

She knocked. No answer. She tried the knob. Locked. Her hands were sweaty, the air in her chest stale. She knocked again, and then, impatient and pushing back panic, she walked into the yard to look over the house. She pushed a giant Scooby Doo out of her way and tried to peek in the big front window, but the house was so dark. It shouldn't have been so dark, she was sure, but then she realized she didn't see Yolanda's car. Her chest felt less restricted —

maybe they all went out. Maybe the house was just dark because nobody was home.

Maybe everyone was dead.

She ran back to the porch and pounded on the door, just pounded and pounded relentlessly because why not? If no one was home, no one would know.

Michael opened the door. Little Mr. O'Lantern. He stood a few steps back from the glass between them, looking up at her in his footie pajamas, crying. Dez opened the screen door, kneeled, and hugged him.

"Hey, hey," she shushed. "You OK?"

Michael didn't say anything. He didn't hug back, either. He was like a terrified little rag doll but warm and wet. She peered past him into the dark house.

"Where's your mom?" she asked him, still down on her knees with her hands around him. He didn't answer. Church the cat startled Dez, dashing out of the house and into the yard through the open front door.

She called into the house, "Yolanda?

Hey, Yolanda? Mark?"

No answer.

She squeezed Michael, then stood and took his hand. He pressed his face to her hip and slid his other hand around her leg. She stepped fully into the house, door wide open behind her, and tried to peer past the open kitchen. She could just see a glint of the glass table.

Dez walked toward the kitchen. A wine bottle rolled back and forth on its side on the counter, wine dripping onto the floor. She looked at the mess, then noticed, just beyond the counter, a bloody baseball bat peeking out from beside a couch.

Dez stopped.

"Hey, Michael," she started, calmly. She lifted him up and sat him on a barstool, facing away from the living room. "Stay right here for one minute, OK?"

Michael pulled Dez back toward him. His crying grew louder, and his wet little hands clung to the arms of her shirt.

"Give me just one second, OK?" she

said, as calmly as she could. "I need to check on something, but I won't leave. Do me a favor and keep looking at the front door, OK? In case of trick-or-treaters, OK?"

She reached awkwardly for a stuffed cat on the floor that looked like Church and handed it to him.

"Hang on to this guy and keep watching the front door, OK?"

Michael let go of Dez and clutched the toy. Dez walked cautiously toward the big sectional couch that surrounded three sides of the glass table. Blood saturated the rug, pooling onto the floor beyond it. The glass was shattered. Movement—what she originally took as a crumpled blanket sopping up the blood—shuddered and rolled. She could make out a head. Then the baseball bat moved, and a figure stepped out of the shadows. The bat swung high, paused, and then rushed directly down into the head. Mark's head.

Dez screamed.

A mass of curls shook, and she

stood eye-to-eye with Yolanda. Yolanda's eyes wandered past Dez, followed by the sound of small feet padding quickly away. Yolanda's face turned haunted. She reached past what had been her husband, pulled a large shard of the broken tabletop free, and pushed the glass into her throat.

Dez stumbled backward, rushed to Michael, grabbed him, and ran out the open front door.

***

Destiny and Michael sat on the floor of the back seat of her Hyundai. Dez's long legs made a bridge over the hump in the floor between seats, and Michael curled up on her belly, still hugging his ratty gray cat to his chest. Dez rested her head on his head, and neither looked up—not even when they both heard the sirens, not even when they could see the red and blue lighting up the car windows above them.

Even then, Dez's mind wandered to high school, to State Route 53, flashing lights bouncing off the hanging side view mirror of her smashed Dodge Colt. Only Dez had been moved — strapped to a gurney and headed toward the open mouth of the ambulance somewhere behind her, waiting to swallow her up and carry her away from the crying, the yelling, the silence.

Colleen Kierney lay face down in the dirt a few yards in front of the Colt, her arms behind her back like they were tied together at the wrist, although they were not.

Dez could just see Jenny Beans's nose poking out of a mass of hair about halfway up the hood. Her arms were behind her, too, and she was still inside the car from the hips down. Her body had made it all the way through the windshield, where she'd been launched from the back seat. She had vomited and had been riding in the middle to get away from the mess, her head on Angie Comer's shoulder.

It looked like Angie might have survived the impact and tried to crawl from the car. Her door was open, her head and left hand on the ground, but the rest of her never made it out of the car. The body of a stranger had catapulted onto Dez's car from the crunched, bloody second vehicle that now looked like it was eating its way up her hood.

Statie headlights flashed against the broken mirror and into Dez's eyes.

No, it was a flashlight. Someone knocked on the window, and Michael tugged Dez's shirt over his eyes.

"Everybody OK in there?" a rushed male voice asked.

Destiny counted to ten, and when Michael joined her at three, she realized she was counting out loud. Both of them seemed calmed by it, though. When she hit 10 and could still see the flashlight, she responded, "We're OK."

It took some effort to get the two of them out of the car. They were really wedged in there, plus Dez's legs had gone a bit numb, and Michael didn't want to let go of her. He cried and balled up tight, digging his little nails into her shoulders and neck to get closer.

Eventually—it felt like hours later, but maybe it was only a few minutes—the two survivors sat on the red swing on the front porch. Michael was in Destiny's lap, the ratty Church lookalike crushed up under his chin.

Dez recognized the uniformed officer from the news footage of Grant Arbogast's break-in. She was glad because surely he would see the connection between the crimes. Dez hated explaining the situation with Michael right there on her lap, but he refused to go with anyone else. She didn't want to let him go, either. He was warm, and he smelled like oatmeal, and making him feel safe made her feel safe. But she wished she didn't have to describe the scene with him on her lap.

Still, it was good to get it out that these deaths—Yolanda and Mark, Grant, Adam and his wife—were connected. It was good to tell authorities that this was all part of a larger problem. The idiot cop didn't believe her, she could tell, but somebody had to see that there was some connection.

Some connection besides Destiny.

The officer had left the two alone on the porch. Then, just as a minivan pulled up, he walked back toward Dez and Michael.

"I think the grandparents are here," he told Dez, all antagonism gone from his voice.

She held Michael tighter, saying, "He can stay with me."

An older couple hurried across the lawn toward them.

"He's pretty shocked," Dez told the officer, desperate. "Might be better if he stays with me."

But by this time, Mark's mother was within eyeshot of her distressed grandson.

"Michael!" she called to him, still a few paces off. "Oh, baby bunny!"

Michael perked up at the comforting sound. He slid off Dez's lap and ran to his grandmother, who scooped him up in a teary embrace. Grampa, moving more slowly with a pronounced limp, finally reached the two and hugged both, closing his big arms around them.

Destiny wrapped her empty arms around her middle, cold without the little boy in her lap. A woman exited the house, walking right past Dez as if she were a ghost. She joined the grandparents and the cop, who pointed her back toward Dez on the porch. Dez shivered, watching Badge-on-Chain retrace her steps to the house.

"Miss Arnold?"

Dez nodded.

"I'm Detective Erasga," she announced without offering her hand. "I'm not sure I'm following the statement you gave." She paused, as if waiting for a reply. Dez didn't know what kind of reply to give, so she stayed silent.

"The statement says you're to blame?"

To blame. Blame. Blame, blame, blame, blame, the word echoed around Destiny's head in Erasga's pinched voice until it didn't sound like a word at all.

Sounded made up.

"Miss Arnold?"

When she didn't get any response, Det. Erasga turned toward the officer and flagged him over. He looked combatively at Dez, and she eyed him back.

"I'm just saying it's all connected," Dez finally commented.

"Two murder-suicides in the same circle of friends in a matter of days, we can see the connection," Erasga responded flatly. "But what exactly happened here—haunted videotapes aside?"

"It's not a videotape," Dez said, exasperated now. That idiot cop had misconstrued everything, she could tell. She took a breath and began her story. "I saw a movie called *Yolanda* appear on our film festival submission site."

Dez saw she had their attention.

"A few days back, when the movie called *Adam* appeared, our judge, Adam Vivod, murdered his wife and killed himself."

Dez checked their level of interest. Still with her.

"When Grant Arbogast finally died, that's when the movie *Grant* disappeared. So, when the movie *Yolanda* appeared, that's when I called. I wanted to talk her out of watching it. But maybe I accidentally convinced her to watch it. I don't know. I told her not to. But I was afraid she was going to anyway, so I came. In case."

Erasga waited, not at all patiently, then held her hands up, questioning. "In case of what?"

Dez gestured to the chaos around them.

Erasga asked, "So there's a movie somewhere that predicted all of this?"

"Yes!" Dez reacted, maybe more excitedly than she meant to. "Maybe. I didn't watch it."

Detective Erasga looked baffled and irritated but not entirely discouraged.

"Can I see it?"

"No," Dez admitted.

"It disappeared," the uniformed officer added with air quotes.

"I bet you can go through the platform and get information on the filmmakers," Dez offered, doing their detective work for them, she thought. She was encouraged by her own good thinking. "Ask about *Yolanda, Adam,* and *Grant.* In the movie *Grant,* there's this actor, and I think it's Grant Arbogast's dad, Donovan Horrocks, so check on that."

Erasga said quietly to the officer, "Did we reach out to Arbogast's father?"

"Dead for years," he responded. "House still belongs to the family, but Mr. Horrocks expired long ago. Ruled a suicide."

The two officers shared a WTF glance.

"He's in the movie, though!" Dez said, but she knew she'd lost them. "It even shows the stash of kiddie porn hidden in the floor!"

They stared at her blankly.

"In the floor of the Arbogast house... or... well... the Horrocks house," she continued.

Erasga's expression didn't change.

"Give us a minute, will you?"

The two officers put a little distance between themselves and Dez. She couldn't hear them. Maybe they were amazed that she knew about what was in the floor. Why hadn't she thought of that earlier?! That wasn't in any of the news coverage — what other details might prove the video told her more than she should know? Dez wondered if there was really a noose in the closet. Maybe she should mention the little girl.

The two officers turned back toward her, still sitting on Yolanda's red porch swing, and she worked to think of the best way to explain the movie better.

"Miss Arnold, I want to thank you for sheltering the little boy until we arrived," Erasga told her. "Seeing what you saw tonight, that kind of trauma affects people differently. I recommend that you talk to a professional. Someone who can help you process the evening. We can recommend some options if you need help finding someone."

Erasga sort of smiled at her, or her expression changed into what was at least softer.

"You're free to go. We'll call you if we need anything," Erasga said finally, walking past her into the house. Dez caught her by the wrist.

"I thought of some more details from the movie," she said. "There's this sad little girl, and a noose in the closet."

Erasga turned back to her and squatted, so she was closer to eye level.

"You should talk to someone," Erasga told her. "But probably not us. There is no porn, no noose, no little girl. This," she motioned over her shoulder, "this is a straight up murder suicide. Domestic concern. Tragic but not terribly uncommon. Certainly not supernatural. You're not to blame. Go home."

Erasga stood, and Dez realized she was still holding her wrist. She let go and then didn't know what to do with her hand.

Erasga walked into the house and Destiny stood but didn't move. She thought about going in to explain again but couldn't bring herself to see what was inside the house. So, she just stood, until she felt warmth around her ankle and realized again how cold she was.

Church rounded her feet, and she was grateful. She bent down, scooped him up, and carried him to her car.

CHAPTER SEVEN

At home, she set Church on the cold linoleum. He made a break for it down the basement stairs, and she felt the emptiness of the kitchen. She didn't turn the light on, she just stood until she felt herself weave a little bit.

She pulled her phone out of her back pocket to text her sister, then thought better of it and set it face down on the counter. She eyed the laptop across the room suspiciously.

No!

To busy herself, she pulled a baggie of meat out of the fridge, a chopping board from above the sink, a cleaver from the drawer, and a Pokémon cereal bowl from the cupboard. She made Church a little feast and turned to the basement steps.

"Don't tell Maude we used her bowl," she called down the stairs. "We'll get you some real food and a real bowl soon."

Dez sat in the complete darkness of the basement, her back against the big freezer Grace had insisted she take. It held three baggies of leftover roast and a single pint of coffee ice cream. It felt cold behind her back, and its hum made her feel alone in the world until a warm little face pushed against her hand. Church purred as he ate, and Dez consoled herself, running her hand down his fuzzy back. She wondered how long they could stay that way.

Staring into the far dark of her own basement, Dez imagined Yolanda cradling Mark, his head a pulpy mess in her arms. Once the imaginary Yolanda began eating away at the slurry of Mark's bashed-in head, Dez knew it was time to go back upstairs.

She made her way up the basement steps to face her real demon, that silver lid that reflected the microwave light back at her to make sure she saw it. She walked toward the laptop, then walked away from it. Then she sat at the table and lifted the lid, shut the lid, and sighed dejectedly. And then it occurred to her, and she flipped the lid open and found the film site.

She hit refresh and scrolled.

She saw it.

Howie

"No, no, no, no, no, no, no," she cried wearily as she said it. She grabbed her phone from the counter and texted him:

Call me right now

Do not go to the movie site

She paced. She screamed. She jumped up and down, up and down. She called him.

"Hey, it's me. Leave me a message, and I'll get back with you."

"Hi. Hi. Hi," she started. "Um. Don't look on the film site. Stay off of it. Call me when you get this."

There was no air, there was no light, and the whoosh whoosh whoosh of her blood filled her ears. She tried to remember how to be calm, and how to think through things. She looked at her phone as if it would tell her.

"God, where does he fucking work?!" she screamed, then closed her eyes, breathed in, breathed out. "Who would even know that I could ask?"

She texted the first person who came to mind, Howie: *Where do you work?*

No response. She doubled over and screamed.

"Stop!" she scolded. "Stop. Stop," more gently. She looked at her phone again for answers, then Googled his name. The first hit was for an obituary, which made her stomach lurch, but that wasn't him. None of them told her anything. She heard herself breathing, whining.

She texted him again: *call me as soon as you can*

She waited one second and texted: *before you do anything else*

Again, she waited one second and called this time.

"Hey, it's me. Leave me a message, and I'll get back with you."

"I'm not being a stalker," she blurted.

"I really, really need to talk to you right now. Right, right, right now."

She paced and moaned anxiously, sat down at the table, and checked the film site.

Howie was gone.

She slammed the lid and stood bolt upright.

"Oh, God."

Silence. No whoosh whoosh whoosh, no hum of the fridge, not even the sound of her own breath until, at long last, she sucked in air, then bent forward at the waist and screamed one long, high scream. It lasted until she had no air left. Then she stood calmly, picked up her keys and phone, and walked into the deepening dark of October.

She stood silently on the sidewalk next to her car and stared at it. Where was she going? Frustrated, she stomped one foot like a child, then stomped another, then stomped up the sidewalk a bit. She squatted down on her haunches abruptly and rocked there, her mind a buzz of energy and nothing. It was dark now and cold. It smelled like dirt and leaves. Like rot. She could hear music somewhere, scary music. A Halloween party.

She collected herself, stood, and walked with quick, powerful steps to her car.

Dez drove too fast, her face hot and her hands clutching the steering wheel desperately, but she moved with purpose, pulling down side streets and ending up in front of the MacGuffin theater. She came to a stop in the exact spot of the first viral video she'd seen.

Like that tattooed man, she stepped out of her car, drawn to this building for answers. She ran — across the street, through the glass doors, up the wide stairs instead of the escalator. She ran toward the box office at such speed and with such a demonic look on her face that she may have terrified the woman at the counter, who flinched slightly.

"Is Joshua Brose here? I really need to talk to him." Dez was out of breath, disheveled, sweaty.

The woman behind the counter, looking startled at the very least, answered: "Joshua ducked out of here early to take his kids trick-or-treating."

Dez stomped her foot, then tried to restrain her desperation.

"Can I call him?"

The woman looked at Dez curiously, maybe cautiously.

"I suppose so..."

After a long, uncomfortable silence, Dez admitted, "I don't have his number." But the woman's reaction — nodding, thinking — felt like doom, so she lied. "Actually, I do. I just don't have my phone on me at this minute."

She could see the woman's discomfort, the frozen ghost of a smile on her face.

"It's an emergency," Dez added, trying to sound as adult, as quietly authoritative as she could. "Yolanda Sykes is dead."

***

It took Joshua Brose almost 45 minutes to get there. By the time he arrived,

Destiny was standing alone near the concession stand, a much-depleted diet beverage sweating in her hands. Tiny plastic pumpkins dangled above a display window showing candies, their boxes and bags all garish colors: orange and brown, red and yellow. Her energy spent, the drowsy smell of popcorn, and the distant, muffled booms from theaters played on her. She was staring zombielike when Joshua came toward her.

"Are you OK?"

That was enough to snap her out of it. She ignored his question.

"Do you know where Howie Jeremy works?"

Joshua looked confused.

"I have no idea."

She'd committed to the wrong choice and waited all this time, wasting whatever chance she had. He had. It was over now. Dez ran her hands through her hair, paused, and then screamed in frustration.

Joshua jumped, looking immediately around the lobby to raise a comforting hand toward surprised moviegoers. He placed the hand under Destiny's elbow and led her toward a table in the corner of the lobby.

It took some time for Joshua to get the whole story from Dez, who was lost in her own failure. It weighed on her, left her slump-shouldered and frowning, staring at nothing. But she did tell him, and telling him made her think again through the details, and that sparked something. Maybe because Joshua didn't dismiss her. He asked questions and paid attention. She wasn't sure he believed her exactly, but he wanted to hear about it. All of it.

When she'd said everything she could think to say, Joshua rubbed his face wearily.

"This is just...fucking insane."

Did she lose him?

"I know it sounds nuts, but I swear to God, it's happening."

"Yolanda knew about this?" he asked.

"She didn't believe it, but she knew," Dez said. "The police don't believe it, either."

Joshua nodded slowly. He ran his

hands through his copper locks.

"Right."

"But," Dez began, her sleuthing instinct warming, "It occurred to me that they might be able to dig into the platform and find out who's posting the movies. I can't see that, but maybe they could."

She pointed at Joshua Brose.

"Maybe you could."

He looked puzzled.

"Maybe," he offered. "I'll definitely try."

He stood as if to go try right then but turned to Dez.

"When you saw the movie title, *Yolanda*—you warned Mark, right?"

Dez stared blankly at him.

"No."

Joshua's face became shocked, maybe hostile.

"Why not?"

He stared angrily at her. She felt the air seep from her lungs.

"Well, I never talk to Mark," she

stumbled.

"What about Michael?"

"He's good," she near-whispered.

"He's good?!!" Joshua shouted. His normally pale face grew red. He threw up his hands, looked around with his mouth open, and repeated, mocking angrily, "He's good."

He looked Dez in the face, stooping down a little so his face was level with hers. It was an angry teacher stance. A cop stance. An accusing parent or loved one stance. She knew this stance.

"He watched his mom bash his dad's head in with a baseball bat. He's hardly good."

She gasped for air, the popcorn smell filling her mouth and coating her throat.

"Couldn't you have just told Mark that you were worried about Yolanda? That you were afraid she might do something crazy?"

She couldn't really see Joshua Brose anymore. She saw yellows and browns, greens and oranges…blue and red.

"I mean, you wouldn't have even had to say anything about the movie."

Teardrops landed on the table in front of Dez's face.

"You could have just made something up, at least, to get Michael out of the house. What if she'd killed him, too?!"

Loud sobs drowned Joshua out. The sudden, unselfconscious sound shocked him into silence, and his eyes circled the room for witnesses. He shrugged with common discomfort at a patron who made eye contact.

Dez cried harder. She wiped her nose and stood up, then said through sobs, her face red and wet, "Can you give me a call if you find anything about the filmmakers?"

"Yes," he said quietly, not warmly but not harshly. "Stay off the site, though, OK? I'll get a hold of Killer Pictures and cancel the festival. Take the site down. Just shut this nightmare down. Finally."

She ignored him and began to watch

her feet make their way across the big, sparkle-strewn squares of the lobby, then tried one last time.

"You have no idea where Howie works?" she asked weakly, without looking back at him.

"I wouldn't even know who to ask," she heard him say. Nodding sadly, she trudged toward the exit. To no one in particular, she said, "He has a dog..."

She made it as far as her car before she broke out again into loud, ugly sobs. And that's how she sat for she wasn't sure how long, in her car in front of the theater, snotty-faced and hot and bawling. She ran dry eventually and just sat and stared, staring but not seeing the tidy, economical car that was parked just ahead of her. Detective Erasga popped efficiently from the car and strode into the theater without Dez's notice.

***

Carrie and Tommy from the prom, Jessica and Roger Rabbit, lingerie-clad men and women Erasga eventually recognized as *Rocky Horror*-esque, as well as garden variety moviegoers queued up. Erasga eyed the room for an available employee, then stepped in front of the line. Holding out the badge around her neck in one hand, she calmly eyed the pink-haired young ticket taker and said, "I need to speak to the manager on duty."

They faltered momentarily, then grabbed a walkie from their podium and called for Joshua.

"Hey, Joshua?" they warned. "There's a cop here to see you?"

The ticket taker smiled awkwardly, almost comically, at Erasga and then slid the officer politely to one side so they could continue helping guests.

Joshua emerged from a room behind the box office and walked toward the detective, hand extended.

"Hello," he said. "How can we help you, officer? Should we talk in my office?"

"Let's talk wherever I can get a look at the website that lists movies for your festival."

Joshua nodded, autumn-colored locks catching the artificial light.

"No need for a warrant," he told her and paused, smiling. She offered no reaction, and he turned, gesturing for her to follow him to an elevator that carried the two above a first floor, its ceiling high enough to accommodate large movie screens, above the second floor where the Lookover Lounge let guests enjoy a cocktail while eyeing those in the lobby below; to the top floor. Here, stone walls bore a wild assortment of framed movie posters, many hidden behind heaps of velvet chairs and rolled banners, scaffolding and ladders, plastic tables and boxes of fake Oscar statuettes, wigs, clown masks, and shadowy memorabilia. It smelled of dust and buzzed with fluorescent lighting.

A child-sized yellow rain slicker hung decoratively on the door of a small room alight with security screens. Erasga instinctively eyed the screens as she walked by. The two moved past to Joshua's office.

He closed the door behind him and asked: "This is about?"

"I'd like to see what the judges see," Erasga told him. "A site or a page with lists of movies that they would watch to, I guess, pick what gets into your festival."

"Sure, sure," he said, nodding. He spun a laptop around on his desk to face them, keyed in a password, and clicked a link. "Here we are. Hmm." He cocked his head, twisted his mouth, clicked around. "Well, that is not working."

He erased the password and tried again. Nothing.

"I was sure this was the password," he said apologetically. He looked down at the screen, back at the detective with his cold green eyes, and shrugged. "It's not really working."

"Is there a helpdesk?" Erasga asked flatly. "Or someone else with access?"

***

Still outside in her car, Destiny roused from her daze and eyed her phone. Resigned, she tapped the screen and brought up the film site.

She scrolled and saw:

Skullfucker
Obelisk
Obstacle Corpse
Dark Garden
Inhuman Resources
Destiny

Dez sighed. She didn't wait long; she could see no reason to, so she clicked the link bearing her name. And though the screen was much smaller now, she recognized his elegant bone structure and sleepy blue eyes immediately.

Handsome Man sat alone on that same living room floor where she last saw him with the sad little girl. His long fingers drummed his knees. An empty glass and a bottle of bourbon sat next to him, and somewhere beyond him, Dez could make out an open closet door where a noose hung motionless.

"Some of us are better off alone," he

said, his voice low, lulling, convincing. He looked directly into the camera, directly at Dez. He reminded her of therapists, their family room styled offices, their soothing tones.

How could he get back into that house? It's a crime scene now. Unless... unless he owns it. But he's dead. Or...

"We can't bond," Handsome Man continued. "We love wrong. Not warmly. Our attention doesn't nourish. It leaches. When people count on us, believe in us..."

He shook his head as if shaking an idea loose.

"Poor Michael," he said.

Dez felt herself gasp, felt the hot tears begin again.

"Poor, poor Michael," he was looking right at her again. "He'd still have a mommy, wouldn't he?"

She squinted and leaned in toward the screen in disbelief. His lovely, knowing face took up almost all the space. She wanted to see what was in there with him.

She wondered who was holding the camera. She wanted to break the idea that there was no camera, that there was no one else there, only this beautiful, terrifying soul and Destiny.

"It's almost as if you were baiting Yolanda to watch that movie," he quietly accused her. "And now... that poor little boy is all alone in this world."

Her breath caught in her chest. Her vision was blurry from tears, she couldn't see the disappointment as it crossed his face, but she could hear it when he spoke.

"Alone and damaged. Just like you."

She looked away from the phone, out the window toward the theater, and managed to finally suck in some air when she heard him say, "Poor Howie."

***

Inside, Joshua was on the phone with the film site help desk. On the other side of the desk, Detective Erasga fondled the soft leather straps on the arms of his desk chair, but her eyes remained on him.

"She says this password isn't working," he said with an apologetic shrug. "Maybe it expired or something."

Detective Erasga smiled impatiently. "Tell her to manually reset the password for you."

He nodded and pointed, *good idea* like. "Can you try resetting the password manually?"

He looked back at Erasga and gave her the thumbs up.

Joshua pursed his lips and shook his head, tapping away at the laptop. "Uh-huh. Mmm hmmm..." He cradled the phone between his shoulder and ear and looked helplessly at Detective Erasga.

"It's just not working."

Erasga sighed, reached across the desk, and took his phone, turning his laptop toward her.

"This is Detective Rochelle Erasga of the Columbus Police Department," she said into the phone. "I need you to walk me through accessing this film site."

From the other end came an unperturbed female voice. "Of course, Detective," she said. "Why don't I access the site from here and share my screen with you?"

"Why don't you?"

"This will take just a second. I appreciate your patience."

***

Handsome Man poured himself a bourbon, set the bottle on the floor next to him, swished the drink a bit, and took a pull. He pointed toward Dez, drink in hand.

"Howie might have ignored the whole thing except for your stories, right?" he asked. "And now, what will you do? Will you go back to being alone?"

He stretched his long legs out in front of him and rolled his head back and forth against the bare wood paneling behind him, like an exaggerated *no*. He took another drink.

"Entirely alone? You should, you know," he said, pointing again. "How many people can you kill — intentionally or not?"

He sighed, and Dez sat, compelled, breathless. The light from the screen reflected off the scar on her wrist, making it glow a deep purple, like a vein.

"Unintentionally is worse. At least if you did it on purpose, you could stop," he said, then leaned in again as if looking her right in the eye. "You can't help it. You're always trying to do the right thing, but you're poison."

He paused, looking into Destiny's soul, it would seem, then finished the thought.

"And so, you kill all your friends. It's the one thing you're good at. It's your art."

Finally, she inhaled — gulped, really. She saw again the wrecked cars, police lights, the wedding ring on the hand pulling her onto a gurney, two bodies on the street, two almost touching each other across the mangled hoods.

And she heard, "And now you've killed Yolanda and Mark."

She looked again at the handsome man. His lovely face on her phone, cheekbones and jaw defined enough to break through the screen. "You killed Howie. Who's next? Who's left?"

The camera pulled back as light fell across Handsome Man from an open door. The light disappeared, and a woman's legs moved between him and Dez. He looked up as if looking into the face attached to that body.

"How was the party?" he asked.

Did Dez recognize that dress? That ugly green dress? The legs stopped for a second, then walked silently into the closet. The handsome man didn't get up but turned his head away from Dez and watched, then turned back to the motionless camera.

"You killed my daughter's only friend at that party."

She'd killed everyone's friends at the party. She'd killed her own friends, killed any chance she ever had of having friends. The closet was dark, but Dez could see a ladder. Was that Elise? Elise Horrocks? Climbing the ladder? Dez held her breath but never looked away, didn't even blink, as Elise put her head in the noose. Dez stared horrified at her phone, only wincing at the snap of the rope as the body's weight hit it. It squeaked with the swing of the corpse.

Handsome Man turned back to the camera and drew a long breath.

"You did that. You killed my daughter."

Dez didn't disagree with him, not out loud, not in any way. She just felt relief, relief that his matinee idol face filled her phone screen again, and she didn't have to see or think about what was behind him or what was ahead of her. What he said barely registered.

"Who's next?"

He leaned in and she tried to pay attention, tried to do as he wanted.

"I will tell you who's next."

He paused. She recognized the dramatic pause. The formality of it, the process, the theatricality soothed her. He wasn't talking to her. This was a movie. He was an actor. No, that couldn't be right.

"Maude is next."

What? What did he say? Oh, no. No, no, no, no, no, no...

***

Joshua leaned in behind Erasga to see the screen as she struggled to read a list of film titles frozen behind a spinning color wheel.

Erasga bristled at his nearness and dragged her finger across the mousepad with no luck. She tapped the speaker icon and then the Safari icon on her phone, squinting at the URL on the laptop to try her luck on the second device.

"The server's just slow at the moment," the understanding voice of the woman trying to help her log in announced. "There's no real cause for alarm as long as you can be patient. Unless you want to just try again in the morning?"

Erasga took a long, impatient breath.

"Let's wait it out," she responded, and Joshua nodded nervously, eyeing the titles that, though grayed out, were not impossible to read:

Skullfucker
Obelisk
Obstacle Corpse
Dark Garden
Inhuman Resources
Destiny

"Do you want some coffee or anything while we wait?" he asked. "A cocktail, maybe?"

Erasga shot him a look, part baffled, part dismissive.

***

"You don't have a daughter I can take from you, so I will take the next best thing," Handsome Man continued. "And then the next. And then the next."

Destiny threw the phone. It hit the passenger window and landed, face up, in the seat beside her. His beautiful blue eyes stared at her from the small screen.

"Or you can kill yourself."

She fumbled for the phone, clicked out of the site, and pulled her legs around the steering wheel to hold in front of her chest. Balled up in her seat, she sobbed into her knees.

In Joshua Brose's office, the computer screen unfroze just as the film *Destiny* disappeared from the site.

"There we go," the helpful voice said. "What do you want to see?"

Erasga leaned in.

"Scroll slowly."

CHAPTER EIGHT

Dez sat that way, the bones of her back starting to feel the chill until Erasga climbed, unsatisfied, into her efficient car and hit the lights. Then Dez sat longer.

The theater was dark, with no trees or leaves to give it a spooky atmosphere, but at least it wasn't trapped behind a mall somewhere in a squat cement wasteland. Dez opened her car door, and the chill slapped her. She slid around the side of the building and grabbed the lowest rung of the fire escape. The cold of the metal bit into her palm as she walked her feet up the wall to hoist herself aboard, then hand over hand, made her way to the roof.

She wondered if it would be high enough. If it wasn't, she'd end up lying in the parking lot below until midday when the theater reopened. Surely, she would bleed out by then. Looking down from the wide, empty roof into the symmetry of the lined parking lot, she felt calm. Hypnotized.

She turned away and sank, her back to the partial wall that surrounded the flat roof. Pulling her phone from her back pocket, Dez scrolled until she found the same photo she'd meant to frame before she got sidetracked.

Maude was pulling a face. Maude was always making a face. You could never get a straight smile out of her for pictures.

Dez attached the picture to a text and wrote: *I love you two more than anything and everything.*

She sat and shivered for some time, but eventually, Destiny Arnold found her resolve and stepped onto the short wall behind her. She took a deep breath, closed her eyes … and heard a dog.

Her eyes popped open.

The dog barked again, and she heard Howie call for Lester.

She nearly slipped off the wall. She

was so thrown, her heart thumping. She stepped back and looked, following the wall around the building, straining to hear, but she only heard her own sloppy breathing. Nothing. Nothing.

And then she saw Lester trotting between two cars on the side of the building. She was crying again and looking for Howie, afraid to hope, but there he was, wearing the same Halloween III shirt she'd pulled over his head earlier that day. God, it felt like days and days ago, but there he was!

She nearly called out but realized she hadn't breathed in who knows how long and needed to take a dizzy step back. Howie! The saucy laugh, the crooked teeth, the velvety torso.

She heard another happy bark.

And Lester!

Elated, she turned to shout over the wall before climbing down—she didn't want him taking off before she could reach him—when she saw another figure emerge from the shadows beside the theater. He wore a hoodie. But that granite jawline she could see even from this distance. Those sandy curls. Even in the dark from four stories away, he was dreamy.

Handsome Man.

Suddenly very woozy, she squatted low and steadied herself. Her eyes swam in her head as if retracing the images. She crawled to see and maybe even hear what went on below her. It could not be the Handsome Man. Maybe it wasn't him. Lester nuzzled his legs, and he bent to pet the dog. No. No way. This wasn't him; it was a coincidence. It was a trick of her mind. How could he be here? Or know Lester? Or Howie?

Then she heard him. Handsome Man pulled a phone from his back pocket, then looked at Howie and said, in that lovely baritone, "She doesn't think we should stick around in case the cop comes back."

Howie nodded, clarifying, "Cop didn't see anything, though?"

"Nothing to see," Handsome Man

dismissed him, tousling Lester's ears.

Dez fell backward onto her ass. She sat. She stared. She didn't even think, not really, just shook her head for a long time. Lester's bark brought her out of it.

Her breathing became calm, her expression serene. She found her phone again, knelt, and filmed the scene below.

***

Minutes later, Howie was driving, Lester snoring in the backseat. Howie's phone, sitting on top of his jacket on the passenger seat, buzzed, which he ignored, but he thought about checking because you never can tell how plans change. One minute, it's just, "Sit in on the jury panel so you can get to know them," and the next minute, it's, "Destiny likes you. Get close to her and see if she's cracking under the pressure." Which was more than he committed to. And no, he was not pulling his weight before, that's true, but he didn't really expect anybody to actually die. He thought they were just trying to ruin Elise's asshole brother's career and make a few movies on this film festival's dime. Jesus, fuck, how were these people so fucking calm about this?

Not much he could do about it now. What would he tell the police, anyway? We scared everybody to death? And what would the team do to him if he did narc? These fuckers were a lot scarier than he realized. When it was over, he would leave her for real this time and move far away where she wouldn't find him or Lester. Too bad about Dez, though.

She was definitely going to die. He could already see her caving to the whole thing this afternoon, and he felt so shitty about it. He kind of rooted for her — it would serve everybody right if the whole big con just exploded in their faces, Dez fucking it all up like some mythic final girl. But Dez was a basket case. She'd be the easiest one to push over the edge.

"That's too bad, eh Lester? You like her, don't you? She's nicer than Mommy, huh?" He reached back to scratch Lester's head and noticed the name on the screen from the last caller: Destiny Arnold.

Howie's expression soured as he glanced back to the road, then back to the phone. An attachment. He fumbled with the phone and tapped to see.

"Fuck."

He looked back to the road, back to the phone, to see Dez's face.

"You're a bad man, Howie."

He swerved, dropped the phone, and picked up speed, though he was now headed to nowhere in particular. He kept his chin above the wheel but groped the floor beneath his feet and his seat for the phone, collected it, and dialed.

"Hey! She's still alive. Dez is alive, and she saw us talking just now. She sent me a video of it!"

A soothing baritone responded, barely ruffled but strategizing.

"Just be calm," he said. "Quiet down and be calm."

"Don't fucking shush me," Howie

demanded. "We are screwed."

"Send it to me," the handsome man told him. "Let me deal with it."

Incensed and more than a little offended, Howie yelled, "I am not sending this to you. We need to contain it, not have it on everyone's phone for the cops to find."

He waited a long time for a reply.

"Hey!" Howie shouted, impatient and aware that he really did want this man to take care of the problem. "What are we doing about this?"

More silence—it made him want to scream. He was racing now, he knew it, but he wasn't even headed anywhere. He smacked his palm against the steering wheel again and again, freaking out Lester, who jutted his head between the seats, barking.

"We should let Elise deal with it."

"No!" Howie commanded. "Let's call Joshua Brose."

"No," was the calm response. "We are not calling Joshua. Joshua is the client. He's not one of us. Joshua Brose is beside the point."

Hot with rage, fear, and that awful feeling of getting caught, Howie gritted his teeth and waited for a plan. The traffic light ahead went yellow, and he slowed to a stop. Where was he? He didn't recognize this neighborhood. The street was empty, the road ahead disappearing into darkness.

"Maybe we just, you know, stop. Right? Just, like, end everything right this second." That could work, right? Howie really thought maybe that could work.

"Everything changes once she's the one behind the camera," the deep, rich voice responded. "Before, she was just crazy. What video? What do you mean, Howie's dead? Where did you get that idea? But now, I exist. She is not crazy, and we are accountable."

"But you said it yourself!" Howie shouted. "We didn't do anything!"

Calmly, the handsome man clarified. "We didn't do anything *illegal*. There's a difference. Do I think we can be arrested for making movies that were so troubling people went mad? No. And that is the stuff of legend if you can't prove it. But do I want people to know that we did it, know who I am, what I look like, and where to find me if they have an issue with our…art? I have a future, Howie. This bullshit will not be the end of that just because you were overconfident that Destiny Arnold wouldn't survive the grief of your passing."

Howie's mouth went dry.

"Where does she live?" the handsome man asked.

Howie nodded. Yes, that was what was needed. He felt a cold calm settle over him. It sickened him but also comforted him, and he turned left at the next stop light to circle back.

"I'll pick you up," he told Handsome Man.

It took maybe twenty minutes to get to him, and Howie had tried to empty his mind. He wouldn't suggest anything, just listen critically to the plan.

"Let me see it," the handsome man said calmly, and when Howie handed over the phone, he watched it just as calmly. In the backseat, Lester harrumphed and buried his nose under his paw. Handsome Man fixed his blue eyes on Howie.

"I told Elise."

"God damn it!"

Handsome Man kind of chuckled. "Dude, she's the boss. She may be fucking you, but she's paying me, and she is not somebody I plan to cross. I don't understand why you don't want her to know. Or doesn't she know you boned the victim?"

"It was Elise's idea," Howie admitted.

"Dude," the handsome man said. "Cold-blooded."

"I know," Howie admitted. He felt heat creep up his throat and face and was grateful for the darkness in the car so no one could see him redden with shame. "Why do I go along with the shit she says?"

"Because people who don't believe they deserve love will do anything to keep it."

"Fuck you. Like you're any better."

Handsome Man chuckled softly, shifted in his seat, and watched the video again, paying little attention to Howie.

"Boss points a camera at me, says 'be convincing' and I excel. Nothing but a gig."

"Why do you do it?" Howie asked.

He turned his eyes back to Howie.

"This whole fucking thing," Howie asked. "Why do you do it?"

"I just like to make movies that have an impact."

***

Howie's faded red Honda Civic rolled quietly to a stop next to Dez's house, right where it had parked earlier that day. Dez wondered if that bothered him at all. If he even thought about it. She waited about a half a block back, her lights out, her engine off. Once he parked, she exited her car and rounded to the trunk.

Dez popped the lid and rifled around, pulling out one tool after another: hammer, wrench, tire iron. She felt the weight of each in her hand, put it back, then settled on the hammer.

"Intentional this time," she said. "Own it."

Ahead of her, Handsome Man left the car and walked gracefully toward her house, but she ignored that. She made her way silently toward the Civic.

She saw Lester's head pop up as she approached, but Howie's eyes were glued to the house. It wasn't until his passenger door opened with a flash of the overhead light and a bing, bing, bing, that he finally took note of the situation.

Lester jumped out, Dez got in, and Howie looked startled to death, white, slack-jawed. He recovered.

"Thank God you're OK!" he yelped, then smiled. "We should get out of here. I'll tell you all about it."

He started the car and began to pull into the road, reaching across to squeeze her leg, then dragging his hand across the seat to pull his phone in the console between them into his lap.

"I was really worried about you!" he continued, laughing nervously.

Dez hit him in the face with a hammer.

He swerved, running his car up onto the sidewalk. Bleeding and shocked, he grabbed for his head.

Dez reached into his lap, lifted the phone, and dropped it in her pocket, then raised the hammer again.

"Wait, wait, wait, wait!"

Outside, Lester barked and circled the car, tail wagging, as Dez's arm and hammer flew up and down, up and down, sometimes catching in meat and requiring a good tug.

Then she opened the passenger door and climbed out, spattered with blood and viscera. She closed the door behind her and took a minute. She took in the night air. It had really gotten cool. She smoothed her hair, wiped her face with her hands, then turned to look at Lester. She rubbed his head. What a good boy! Dez readjusted the hammer and walked toward her house.

Handsome Man was sitting in the dark at her dining room table, right where she'd sat and watched him that very first time.

"Hello!" That voice—familiar, dreamy, knowing.

Dez gripped the hammer.

He leaned forward, his lovely profile catching moonlight through that window Grace had uncovered.

"You are quite a mess, aren't you?" he chuckled.

She took a few confident steps across the linoleum, and he asked, "What did you do to Elise Horrocks, anyway?"

She stopped.

"Fuck you."

He pointed up and down at Destiny. "This looks pretty bad for you—assuming that's not your blood." He smiled, smug but still lovely. "You know that makes you the only one of us who's actually committed a crime, right? So, what are you going to do now? Murder all of us and explain to the police that a haunted movie made you do it?"

He shook his head. She looked into his lovely face, his eyes an unreasonable blue even through her dark house.

"Do you want to face that? Again? All those people judging you because you killed so many people," he stopped, shook his head laughing. "Again!"

She was unperturbed, but if he noticed he didn't let on. He stood, the full length of him impressive. He laughed and stepped toward her.

"That look in your sister's eye—pain, pity, shame," he shook his head and walked closer. She realized how cold the house was when she felt the heat of him near her, and she wondered what he smelled like, but all she could smell was Howie's blood, sticky and human, in her hair and on her clothes and on the hammer.

"You still only have one real choice here," he purred. "You always have. It's what you should have done years ago. End everyone's misery. Protect the people you love from your poison. Take your own life."

Moonlight danced in his hair, and it saddened her that he'd never make another movie.

"There's nothing else you can do," he said, quietly, certainly. "You know it, and I know it."

"No offense," she told him. "But this has nothing to do with you."

She swung the hammer.

What a mess a hammer makes, she thought, looking at his body, stretched out from mid-kitchen into the dining room and pooling blood. Church nuzzled her leg, and it dawned on her. She opened the back door, and a grateful Lester bounded into the scene.

They looked so cute she snapped a picture.

"Who's hungry?"

It took a while—the handsome man was a long slab of puppy chow—and the job was hardly finished. There was still an awful lot of blood to clean up, plus Howie in the car. But she had two pets now. They were well-fed, and that freezer was finally put to good use. Dez wiped herself clean, more or less, with a towel from the drier and put on warm, soft sweats and socks. She went to throw the filthy stuff in the washer and fished Howie's phone from her pocket.

She just made out the vanishing text. Elise asked: *Is she dead yet?*

CHAPTER NINE

Elise was back at the theater, in the parking lot, waiting for Howie to respond.

"Do I do a Dez and Yolanda video or just Yolanda?" Tattoos was asking. "We know Yolanda's dead for sure. Maybe just go with that one?"

Elise checked her phone again. Still no word. It was so like him to leave her hanging. Did she have to do every goddamn thing? She drew an angry breath. "Just do the Yolanda video for now until we know for sure Destiny Arnold is dead."

In the distance, Howie's car rolled into the parking lot. Tattoos pointed.

"Thank Christ," she said.

The car rolled to a stop at the far end of the lot and turned its lights off. The space between them was empty, with little pools of light from lamp posts making the void between them seem darker.

"Why did he stop back there?"

She waved at the car, flagging him over.

"Maybe to stay out of the shot?" Tattoos offered, and Elise nodded.

"Go ahead."

Tattoos cleared his throat, lifted his phone, and recorded.

"Another day, another bloody death attached to the Murder and Mayhem film festival," he said, sneaking around the theater parking lot as if he were trespassing. He held the phone close to his face and said, "Yolanda Sykes came home from trick-or-treat tonight and killed her husband and herself right in front of her 4-year-old."

***

Far behind him, Destiny Arnold snuck into the shot. She was wearing an oversized sweatshirt, a stocking cap hiding the blood still sticky through her hair. She ducked behind a dumpster, then into some trees, then into the shadows at the far end of the building.

Joshua exited those same shadows and walked quietly to Elise just as Tattoos finished filming. Joshua threw him a sarcastic thumbs-up and said, "Do me a favor. Upload it upstairs so you can swipe the security cameras." Then, loudly and more unhappily toward Elise. "And from now on, make sure I know you're filming back here."

Joshua looked angrily toward Elise.

"That's the kind of information I should have."

He walked Tattoos to the theater door, and the younger man asked, "What are we hiding? We didn't kill anybody."

"You do understand publicity, right?" Joshua asked, seething. "I mean, that's your whole schtick, isn't it?"

He unlocked the door, not more than a few feet from where Dez hid in the shrubbery. Joshua held the door open for Tattoos, who looked back and asked, "How long?"

"At least the last hour," Joshua answered, letting the door go. Then he thought better, snatched the door open again, and called in, "Then just turn the cameras off altogether to give us whatever time we need to get out of here."

A wicked smile crossed Dez's face.

Joshua stalked back to Elise, his shiny shoes clicking on the pavement. Dez thought magicians probably moved more stealthily. Quietly, staying close to the building, Destiny slunk through the shadows toward them.

"How much clearer can I be?" he fumed, walking toward her.

"What?" Elisa said, mockingly? "Something wrong, boss?"

"What the fuck, Elise? I told you this was over; you and your demented Argentos were supposed to stop."

"Oh, quit being such a baby. You wanted Yolanda gone. It was my favor to you, really."

Joshua ran the last few steps, looking

to Dez like his head would burst.

"What are you even saying?!" he whisper-yelled between gritted teeth. Dez hoped the rest of the conversation would stay audible.

"Oh, I'm sorry, you wanted to protect Yolanda? Did you warn her, Joshua? Did you take down the site?" Elise smiled wickedly. "No. You wanted her to watch, you coward."

Joshua grabbed Elise by both arms and shook her.

"Her little boy was there!"

"Are you crying? Jesus, man."

He hung on.

"You have gone too far," he said, quietly through his teeth. "It ends now."

Elise's expression slid from shock to playful contempt, and she tipped her head to one side.

"Or what?"

He let go, repulsed.

"Is that a real question? What is wrong with you?"

"No, seriously," she smiled. "What is it you think you're going to do about it?"

"You know the police were just here, right?"

She rolled her eyes. "If you were going to talk to them, you'd have done it already. And, as I have said, lo these many times, what are you going to say? What have we done?"

He pressed his hands hard against his eyes and laughed miserably.

"I cannot believe this is happening," he whined, looking up. "When Grant came to me and said he was trying to reconnect with his kid sister, would I listen to her pitch—"

Elise interrupted.

"You're the one who told me that this festival would sink the entire business unless somebody with a killer instinct stepped in."

He scoffed. "I meant me!"

Elise snickered a little mockingly.

"And I did not literally mean 'killer'!"

"You're as guilty as anybody," she

told him.

Beyond them, Destiny peaked out from behind a bush.

"Elise," he paused with an angry chuckle. "I thought your idea was insane and stupid. 'Movies so scary they kill you.' But, I figured, what could it hurt? Can you believe that? Those were literally the words in my head when I hired you."

"You had no faith," she responded flatly.

"I didn't know you were a fucking psychopath! I didn't think it would really happen!"

Joshua was spitting and flailing his arms, but Elise was unflappable. Dez was almost impressed.

"I told you I was good at it. Honed this talent long ago," she smiled.

Unseen, Destiny peeked out.

"You and your psychotic lap dogs killed a lot of innocent people!" Joshua announced dramatically. Dez could almost picture a fluttering cape.

"Did not," Elise responded like a brat. "I made scary movies. It's a gift. Just ask my dad."

She laughed.

"Oh, wait, you can't. It's hardly my fault how people react to scary movies."

"Why even target that poor Vivod guy?"

"We needed a test run," she said. "Plus, I can't bear a nice guy, let alone a happy couple."

Joshua Brose actually began to pull his hair out. Dez had heard the phrase before, but never actually seen it happen. He calmed himself to a degree.

"Wow. I knew you hated your brother, but you just hate everyone, don't you?"

Her sudden smile was shocking, demonic.

"Elise, you have more than made your point. You know what scares people."

Destiny inched closer. She stayed close to the bushes, and Joshua Brose's body obscured Elise from her view. Dez realized suddenly who he reminded her of. Not a magician. He looked like a grown-up, well-manicured, bearded Chucky doll. Friends to the end. She tried to picture him in denim overalls.

"And the festival that used to hemorrhage cash is notorious enough to guarantee yearly pilgrimages from the dirtbags who love this kind of shit," Elise said. "And all we did was make really effective movies. Where's the crime in that?"

Joshua stepped in close and hissed, "And now we're done."

Dez got brave, slinking a little farther toward the parking lot to get a better view. Elise looked different, more sophisticated. She still wore her hair in bangs, though they seemed somehow more severe now.

"No."

Oh, his face was so purple! What a fun color with that hair!

"What's the point of continuing? This is reckless, Elise."

"None of that matters if Destiny Arnold doesn't kill herself," Elise said.

"Jesus Christ, why not?!" Joshua sounded more exhausted by the argument than angry or curious.

Elise paid little attention to him. As she began waving with big, broad sweeps at Howie's car out by the dumpster, she explained, "She's a murderer."

"Sorry?" Joshua's interest seemed piqued.

"She got drunk and killed a carful of innocent people, and nothing happened to her. Bodies were everywhere: on the street, across the hood. A lot of bodies. My best friend's body."

"Oh my God, Destiny Arnold killed your best friend." Joshua sounded genuinely shocked by the news.

"Right? So, fuck her," Elise said, turning to look at Joshua. "I was actually supposed to be in that car, but she left me behind."

"Feels like you should probably thank

her then, not kill her," he suggested.

Rage crossed Elise's face. "I am not taking life advice from a middle-aged man who hasn't yet mastered birth control."

Oh, that was a good one. Dez smiled. She hated to interrupt, but she was close enough now, so she coughed to draw attention to herself as she stepped fully onto the sidewalk.

Joshua stepped in front of Elise and pointed her toward the bushes, where she hid with some trouble. He called out: "Dez! I'm surprised to see you here."

Dez ran up to him, giddy almost. She left some space between herself and Joshua because she could smell the metallic human stench that clung to herself, and she didn't want him to notice it. You wouldn't know that smell from movies. It smells thick and meaty, kind of salty. Dez had all but forgotten that smell.

"Mr. Joshua!" she beamed. "So glad I caught you."

She stopped for a second, smiling like

a loon.

"I left my phone," she said finally.

Joshua looked relieved and also annoyed.

"Where did you leave it?"

She pointed up. "On the roof."

Joshua followed her finger skyward, then looked back at Dez, curious.

"How did you manage that?!"

"Nutty, right?" she answered. "Too, too nutty!" She stared at him, smiling like a clown.

There was a long, terribly awkward pause. Joshua's gestures seemed to stutter, his shoulders shrugging slightly, his head giving just the smallest shake. This was a man facing a woman who did not pick up on cues, and he seemed to struggle with exactly what to do next, and the thought made Dez smile brighter.

"Well, the theater is closed right now," he said finally, taking an authoritative but calming tone.

"Can't you let me up there?"

He held up his hands and looked at his watch, but before he could answer, she said, "I mean, it's either now or later, right? We're here now. Let's do it now. Right?!"

Oh, her mood was so light, so bouncy.

***

Joshua pulled the keys out of his pocket again, and the two entered the building. From her hiding spot, Elise could hear him ask, "What were you doing on the roof?" just before the door banged shut.

Elise peeked out of the bushes. She was anxious, not sure what to do for the first time in a long, long while. She waved again toward Howie's car. Nothing. God damn that useless man. Irritated, she tiptoed to Joshua's car and tried to get inside to hide, but it was locked. She could hear Joshua and Dez on the roof, their voices muddy but agitated. And then she heard, clear as a bell, "No! No, no, no, no, no!"

Joshua dropped to the pavement in front of Elise. His body popped, splattering her with hot blood. She startled and stared, too shocked to scream. She didn't move until he whimpered.

Oh, God.

Shaking, Elise looked around her and took a step toward him, but the sound of feet on the fire escape sent her panicking back to her spot in the bushes. When she could no longer hear footsteps, she strained to pick up where Dez might be.

In Dez's hand, Joshua's keys dangled and jangled. Elise quietly exhaled all the air she had, got as small as possible, and watched Destiny Arnold almost skip toward Joshua's body.

Then Elise heard the smack of the theater door, and as Dez's head turned, Elise realized her dopey but loyal friend Everett, who'd sat so still while she drew on all those tattoos, was going to die.

Elise shrunk and watched the episode through the greenery. The parking lot light post dropped a perfect spotlight over her doomed friend as he stopped halfway between Elise's bush and Dez. He just stood there like an idiot. Before he took another step, Dez strode toward him, sliding several keys between her fingers as she moved. She planted those keys in the side of his throat and yanked them back out, stepping comically out of the way of the blood spray.

Jesus!

Poor Everett. Elise watched the confusion in his face turn to terror, and she was surprised by a deep desire to let him see her, just so he wouldn't feel alone in his last moments.

The beep of a fob interrupted her sorrow, and she watched Dez get into Joshua's car. Finally, Elise inhaled, breathing steadily but calmly. She would not give away her position.

The car started almost soundlessly, but the lights were blinding. Elise crouched lower in her spot.

***

The engine purred more than it revved. The steering wheel was covered in soft leather straps. The seat warmer was already on, and it made Dez realize that she was a little chilly. As she buckled up, she remembered the time, after the first meeting of the whole Mayhem jury team —all dead now except for Dez—that she insisted on driving this very car back from Larry's Den, the campus dive where they drank Natty Light pitchers for three dollars apiece. It was like a bet that she wouldn't take, guzzling Diet Pepsi instead. Everyone had mocked her for forcing herself into the driver's seat. Even Howie.

Oh, Howie.

She put Joshua's Lexus in gear and drove as fast as it would take her into the building in front of her.

Joshua's body sort of squished beneath the weight. She'd felt the satisfying thump thump of him. The real gift waited for her when she opened her eyes, though, and met Elise's. Well, one of them. Elise's face was in profile, pressed to the center of the badly cracked windshield.

"Wow," Dez said, dizzy. "Haven't

been in a car accident in a while."

She looked around the front seat. Looked at herself as well as she could. Rolled her head from side to side to check for injury. She looked through the windshield at Elise. Nothing moved. No sign of life.

Dez let herself out the driver's side door and examined the car, Elise's body pinned between the hood and the theater, a spray of leafy green on either side of her like some kind of ornamentation.

"Hey!" Dez said, suddenly cheerful. "It's like *Final Destination*! I guess you *were* supposed to be in the car with us that night."

Dez nodded, rolled her neck one more time, and then walked back to Howie's car, which was still parked behind the dumpster.

It took a while—dead bodies are so heavy!—but the job was done. The sun reddened the sky over that looping fire escape ladder as blood-covered, weary, contented Destiny Arnold walked toward the street. It was probably three miles to her house, and it would be fully dawn by the time she got there. Maybe she could get a couple hours of sleep before Lester and Church needed breakfast.

Behind her, the chrome on Joshua Brose's bumper caught the new light.

She'd kept the scene as close as possible to her memory of the wreck that inspired it. She'd arranged the bodies of Howie, Elise, Tattoos, and Joshua in and around the two blood-spattered cars.

Once she released the man bun, Tattoos had the hair for it, his nose just barely poking out toward Elise, of course, who was already halfway up the car hood. Then it was just dragging the pretty flattened and very sloppy Joshua over to the back seat to hang half in, half out of the car.

And then Howie, hands behind his back, head split wide open. Colleen Kierney might have liked him.

Dez looked back at her work. She smiled.

"I enjoy a solid reboot."

Headed for the road and home, Dez

pulled her phone out and texted Grace.

Made some new friends. You and Maude should come meet them.

She attached photos of Lester and Church and hit send.

Hope Madden is an award-winning writer, filmmaker, and film critic based in Columbus, Ohio. Her novella, *Roost,* published in March of 2022 with Off Limits Press. Her short story "Aggrieved" is featured in the 2022 feminist horror anthology *Incubate,* from Speculation Publications. Her short "Meat" is part of the Wicked Shadow Press 2024 anthology *Flash of the Dead: Requiem.* She has two additional shorts forthcoming with Wicked Shadow Press: "Clown Wanted" for their 2024 anthology *Flash of the Dead: Halloween,* and "Customer Service" in their anthology *Petting Boo,* also due out in 2024. Her second novella, *Killer Pictures,* is set for a 2025 release date from World Castle Publishing. Her first feature film, *Obstacle Corpse,* is now streaming on Amazon Prime.

www.ingramcontent.com/pod-product-compliance
Lightning Source LLC
Chambersburg PA
CBHW032002170626
46807CB00006B/2603